A Novel

We agreed to meet just here

Scott Blackwood

New Issues Poetry & Prose

Western Michigan University
Kalamazoo, Michigan 49008

Copyright © 2009 by Scott Blackwood. All rights reserved.
Printed in the United States of America.

First Edition, 2009.

ISBN-10: (cloth) 1-930974-80-9
ISBN-13: (cloth) 978-1-930974-80-7

Library of Congress Cataloging-in-Publication Data:
Blackwood, Scott
We Agreed to Meet Just Here: A Novel/Scott Blackwood
Library of Congress Control Number: 2008926637

Art Director: Tricia Hennessy
Designer: Amanda Schwarz
Production Manager: Paul Sizer
The Design Center, Frostic School of Art
College of Fine Arts
Western Michigan University

This book is the winner of the Association of Writers & Writing Programs (AWP) Award for the Novel. AWP is a national, nonprofit organization dedicated to serving American letters, writers, and programs of writing. Go to www.awpwriter.org for more information.

This book is a work of fiction. Names, characters, places and incidents either are products of the author's imagination or are used fictitiously. Any resemblance to actual events or locales or persons, living or dead, is entirely coincidental.

A Novel

We agreed to meet just here

Scott Blackwood

NEW ISSUES

For Tommi

I feel sometimes as if I were a child who opens its eyes on the world once and sees amazing things it will never know any names for and then has to close its eyes again. I know it is mere apparition compared to what awaits us, but it is only lovelier for that. There is a human beauty in it. And I can't believe that, when we have all been changed and put on incorruptibility, we will forget our fantastic condition of mortality and impermanence, the great bright dream of procreating and perishing that meant the whole world to us. In eternity, this world will be Troy . . . and all that has passed here will be the epic of the universe, the ballad they sing in the streets.

—Marilynne Robinson, *Gilead*

I'm going away
Where you will look for me
Where I'm going you cannot come
No one's ever gonna take my life from me
I lay it down
A ghost is born

—Wilco

Men die because they cannot join the beginning and the end.

—Alcmaeon, Greek physician, 6th century B.C.

Words Fail.

—from an anonymous letter
found at Jonestown

I

1

The river winds through the cedar and oak clotted hills west of our city. Along its limestone bluffs, where Tonkawa Indians once lived, now sprawl lavish Mediterranean-style homes. Gazing from the terraced deck of one of these, you'd see our city's earnest skyline to the east, a half-dozen crane arms hoisting new bones alongside the pink granite dome of the state capitol. To the north, the University Tower, its clock face and observation deck, from which a man once shot and killed fourteen people. Others have leaped from the tower, coaxed by the dizzying voice of the ground, some leaving behind shoes neatly paired on office window ledges, notes folded in pockets: I didn't fall, I wasn't pushed, I jumped. *You might even hear that same dizzying voice now, standing at the terraced deck's railing one early August afternoon, watching a paddleboat move upriver past Deep Eddy swimming pool, pale green and winking in the heat. On the hill beyond, the peaked roofs of our craftsman-style homes, our shadowed porches and lawns.*

And in one backyard, Winnie Lipsy stares up into the gnarled branches of an oak, where her eight-year-old son Isaac sits. Too high, *she says.* Come down now. *She can't help but raise her arms above her head as if she too were climbing.* Come down now. *And later, when we hear about Isaac's fall from that tree, his arm broken in three places, we remember Winnie's self-contained silences at our parties and homeowners' meetings, gaps between words which we anxiously fill with talk of rising property taxes, crepe myrtles, and perennial beds, and we think of this as her comeuppance. At the hospital, some of us embrace her, feel her body at first stiffen then give way a little, like a loose hardwood plank beneath your foot. We talk of our own sons' and daughters' broken bones, their near misses, their current troubles. Winnie listens, her face taut, expressionless, and we think of deer we sometimes still see along our greenbelt standing in groves of cedar, motionless, testing the air. We imagine she is thinking, not of her son, but of her long ago given-up daughter, and for a moment, she gives way to us, and we can feel the morning-dark quiet of our houses just before the children wake up, just before our hearts are gripped with doubt. We want to absolve her of all the lies she will tell herself and her children because we wish to absolve ourselves. We later come by Winnie and Dennis Lipsy's house to deliver jelly beans and cookies, to sign Isaacs's cast with our looping scrawls, and, like the dizzying voice of the ground, we say,* See how small a thing it is that keeps us apart?

***

For decades, our children have skinned their noses and chins on Deep Eddy Pool's shallow bottom. NO JUMPING the white painted letters on the side say, yet they dive, jackknife, cannonball, and shot-in-the-heart-gunfighter fall into its spring-fed water. Scars stretch on skin until almost imperceptibly they become our children's grown faces. The pool, too, is scarred from one hundred years of floods: granite blocks from burst dams have scored it; ancient uprooted cypresses have hammered its plaster sides. After one flood in the 1920s, a great hole was gouged in the bottom. The pool's owner, a former circus promoter, took the opportunity to dig the hole even deeper and line it with canvas. He constructed a sixty-foot platform for Lorena and her diving horse, who appeared nightly at 8:05 sharp. We've seen pictures of her up there on her horse, Mumford, staring down into the great watery wound below.

For three summers, Natalie Branch was our pool lifeguard. She wore an old broad-brimmed white hat, the kind a fifties movie star might wear, while perched on her platform overlooking the pool. We coveted Natalie's smooth pale skin, her wide hips and large breasts, so unlike the tan boyish bodies of the other girls who worked the pool. We watched with a kind of awe across the water as she gazed down between her knees at a knot of rule-breaking teenagers, some of them our own sons and daughters, their faces repentant. Later, she'd wave them over and they'd talk excitedly with her, forgetting themselves, their limbs intertwining lazily with the legs of her platform. We understood. Sometimes we pretended Natalie was our girl. So what did Natalie have to say? *we'd quiz our children on the walk home, our secret hearts clenching. Vacationing in Colorado or on South Padre Island, we'd suggest sending Natalie a postcard and our children would give us sheepish looks and go silent, as if they suspected. And sometimes we'd see Natalie standing in line just outside the pool at Jim-Jim's Fruit Ice stand, talking to college boys about a local band or a foreign film showing at the University (Almodóvar, a name we rolled in our mouths like a lozenge). She'd let the college boys buy her mango ices and then dismiss them, all the same, with her wide, canted hips, promising only that she'd be at the pool again tomorrow, the white hat askew on her head, fingers winding and unwinding her tethered whistle. Some of us wanting nothing more than to drunkenly fall upon Natalie in the darkened backseats of our Volvos and SUVs some night after she'd swum her mile. Smell chlorine on her skin. Wear her wide-*

brimmed hat low over our eyes, as she does.

And sitting by the pool one late afternoon in July, Winnie Lipsy had looked up from her book to see Natalie's wide-brimmed hat being swept across the water by a gust of wind. It caught against the chain-link fence. Maybe Winnie thought about retrieving it. Rose off her towel. Looked across the pool to where Isaac was but couldn't find him. Her heart stuttered. A dark shape was submerged near the lap lanes. People underwater can't breathe *is what she thought. For an instant, she imagined the pool emptied, EMTs crouched around her son, a puddle spreading on the concrete. But then Isaac's head poked to the surface and she shoved the image aside, as any of us would. Natalie came for her hat and smiled at Winnie as she passed. Another wind gust and Natalie clamped the hat on her head with both hands and pretended to fly over the shallow end of the pool, soaring over a few of the small children, who giggled and splashed. And before Winnie made her way to her son on the other side of the pool, before she touched his head like a talisman, she might have thought how our Natalie was everything she was not at nineteen: sensuous, funny, unselfconscious, unafraid.*

* * *

In late August, the sun hammers our city flat and listless. The river has a fetid smell. At home, we sweat and bicker with our children returning from the last week of camp or just-ending summer jobs. We walk our dogs, who, grown sullen from the heat, have forgotten the nutrias swimming along our riverbank. We visit the pool in the early evening, play keep-away and Marco Polo with our children, and look for Natalie, but she's nowhere to be seen. A few of us ask an acne-faced boy at the front counter if she's sick. He shrugs, says he doesn't know. Do you work here? *we want to ask. Tomorrow, she will be back, we tell ourselves, already wistful. But then we see her outside the fence, locking her bike to the railing, and realize our Natalie has only swapped shifts. We breathe easier.*

The pool shows movies on Thursday nights. Creature from the Black Lagoon. Jaws. *From our porches, we can hear children's collective screams. When they first started the movies years ago, Ruth Dodd heard the screaming and called the police.* Didn't they tell you about the movie night? *someone asked. Yes, she said, but what did that have to do with all those awful screams?*

On movie nights, we make drinks, sit on our porches and wait for them. The joy and terror in those voices. The hairs rising on the backs of our necks. The night, sharpened.

And then, just before Labor Day, the pool is closed for repairs. We stare in disbelief at the sign on the gate, the pale green water winking up at us below. Curse under our breath. Our children protest. Older ones look at one another, say, There's more than one way to skin a cat, *certain that only they could be clever enough to come up with such a macabre expression. So they say it again.*

The night is clear. Heat radiates off our streets and houses, back into space. We sit on our porches and look at the stars and try to recall constellations. Cassiopeia is one. Pleiades, the seven sisters. We try not to think of Natalie. We remember the TV weatherman saying that relief is on the way.

2

Dennis was gone the afternoon Isaac fell from their backyard oak and broke his arm. The break was serious—a compound fracture—so the doctors rushed him into emergency surgery. Winnie called Dennis but couldn't reach him. He was visiting Sonny Farbrother, an elderly client who lived in Dripping Springs, he'd told her, and the cell phone was out of range. But, in fact, he'd followed Natalie Branch into a movie at the Paramount Theater downtown that afternoon and turned off the phone. When Dennis finally got Winnie's messages and called her at the hospital, she was frantic, her voice sharp with accusation and hurt. *She had called and called, for God's sake. Where was he?* Dennis wasn't sure anymore. He was thirty-eight years old. He was in decent shape, though recently his ankles and knees had begun to give him trouble when he ran. He loved his wife and son in an oddly fluid way, as if he was rising and falling through an uneven water table. Sometimes, a kind of pressure built up in his ears and he would wake up beside Winnie at night, restless and agitated. He grew distracted at his law office and took on too many clients, or forgot to collect from ones he had. Winnie, out of frustration, had even started posing as a collection agent and calling some of them at home. Dennis's clients often wanted him to renegotiate their already-lived lives. Challenge child-custody agreements, revise wills, address long-term grievances. It was nearly always too late, though they wanted him to say otherwise. Like the Cretan Liar, he knew that everything he told them was both true and false.

Can you regain custody of your kids? Sure. But at what cost? The law is only a powerful fiction, he wanted to tell them. Your children won't be more yours than before. Maybe less. But his clients came to him in love with possibility. Dennis understood.

***

At the Pattersons' Fourth of July party last summer, Dennis had made a mistake. He was fixing margaritas in the kitchen when Natalie came in from playing volleyball in the backyard. Her face was flushed and he could smell citronella oil and sweat on her skin. Her bare feet were covered in sand. She grabbed a beer from the fridge. Cut her eyes at him. "You won't tattle, right?" The sun had brought out her freckles. She wobbled a little. He could hear volleyballers shouting outside. Natalie's mother was out there somewhere. "I'm taking the day off from tattling," Dennis said. She smiled. Drank down half the beer. Dennis sliced limes. They talked about movies she'd seen that summer. Jean Cocteau's *Beauty and the Beast* was one. When Belle gets to the castle, Natalie told him, pale arms come out of the darkness and hold onto her. "Suspend your disbelief," Natalie said in mock-dramatic voice, and with one disembodied hand, she demonstrated on herself how they did this, how the hands ran through Belle's hair and along her shoulders, how Belle turned and twisted but couldn't get away.

"Those arms stay with you," Natalie said. She drank the rest of her beer. She teetered dizzily there in front of him, then grabbed his shoulder to steady herself. "Whoa," he said. The muscles in her face slackened. She was looking at him, but looking past him, too. She told him the ending of the movie was all wrong. Belle chooses one thing and ends up with another. "When Greta Garbo saw it, you know what she said? She said:

give me back my beast."

There was a dusting of sand under Natalie's chin. What was he thinking when he lifted his hand to brush it away? Of the dent in Natalie's forehead made by the corner of the Dodds' picnic table when she was four and the way the skin reddened there when she was angry. Of her father, who lost her in a child custody case when she was seven. Of the summer-roughened bottoms of her feet headed up the pool steps.

Outside, laughter. Then someone's kid was crying.

Natalie took his hand in hers and held it to her cheek. His head filled with water. He would kiss her. No one would know. Her wide eyes, erotic and sad. Resigned to something. To him? The late afternoon sun fingered along the floor. Dennis found his other hand, the one with the lime halves, touching Natalie's shoulder. She pulled away. Limes tumbled to the floor. Natalie turned, opened the fridge, went up on her toes for another beer.

"It was a mistake," he said to her back.

The crying kid came through the back door, followed by his mother.

Later, Dennis would see Natalie and her mother talking with Winnie in the backyard, the lime-moist smudge of his hand still visible on Natalie's sleeve.

3

If you had lived long on our street, and drunk late at our parties, you would know that before retiring and moving to Texas, Odie Dodd had been a government physician in Georgetown, Guyana. Squawking through the hole in his throat where his larynx had been before the cancer, Odie would have told how Jim Jones had asked him to the People's Temple to vaccinate the children. How malaria, cholera, bacterial meningitis slept in the jungle underbrush. How his truck had overheated along the rutted jungle road and he'd arrived a half-day late. How he was the first to find the bodies, though. Families. Limbs intertwined. Mothers sprawled over children as if sheltering them from some imminent hardship. Scattered on the dirt around them, Dixie cups that had held the grape punch and cyanide. And already, of course, the smell. The uninterrupted whine of insects. At the party, Odie's hand would flatten his silver comb-over, and he'd say, with his typical British understatement, that he hadn't known where he was for a time. That he'd wandered outside the compound and crouched in the shade of the jungle, the insect whine growing louder. In his daze, he glanced up into the canopy and for a moment it seemed it would descend on him. His scalp prickled. He called out. The feeling, he would say, was as in a dream when you know a terrible thing is about to happen but you are helpless to prevent it. But of course the thing had already happened. And then, if Odie had sipped enough scotch, and his wife Ruth had not yet touched his elbow to leave, he would have pulled you aside and asked the question he always asked of us: why was he spared? *Later it would occur to you, as it did to Dennis, that Odie had not been spared. And sometimes, when you are at the edge of sleep, witnessing calamities befall your children or your own can't-find-the-brake veering into oncoming traffic, Odie's fleshy hole appears.*

The summer before, when Odie's backyard mangoes ripened and fell, we watched the grackles tear at them and said, he is dying. *Dennis's son Isaac remembered Odie plucking the fruits in the evening, the fleshy wedges Ruth would slice and chill for our Fourth of July block parties.*

We watched Ruth's rigid steps to the mailbox, the weekly arrival of the yardman, to rake and bag leaves, shovel away rotting mangoes. When Ruth's sisters came down from Ft. Worth, we supposed the doctors wanted to remove more of Odie's organs but hoped he would put a stop to it, afraid we would see in his clinging our own graceless last hours. Those of us who had seen Odie and Ruth on the front stoop or climbing into Odie's van for doctor visits felt the exhausted tension between them. Averted eyes. Slumped shoulders. The living grappling with the dying.

So we argued with our sons and daughters over unfinished yard work and waited for Ruth to tell us the news. To our surprise, no calls came. No family caravan of cars appeared. A few of us called. Did they need anything? *No, a nice private nurse came to see them twice a week.* Would they let us cook them a meal or two? *Nothing agreed with Odie was the trouble. The medication was hard on him.* His body is shutting down, *we said, almost approvingly. And then, early last November, we heard his records playing through our open windows at night, just as we had when we first moved here, before our street joined the freeway access road. Now as before, above the ether-whisper of our TVs, we heard scraps of Gershwin, Ella Fitzgerald's "Love is Here To Stay."*

When, last April, Ruth called to say Odie was gone, Dennis—in the same barely audible voice that he used in our living rooms to explain probated wills and community property—told her how sorry he was. Did she want him to make the funeral arrangements? A pause and a gathering of breath. Lord, I don't mean dead, *she said, laughing, then, catching herself.* He's wandering about.

That evening, Dennis gathered us in Ruth's living room, most still in work clothes, a few women corralling children in the dusky front yard. Ruth, unable to hold her hands still, told us the medication must have taken Odie out of his head. Before, she had always coaxed him back inside. The police, she said, had taken a report but nothing could be done until morning. What ditch will he be in by then? *she'd snapped at Dennis, who stood as he usually did, slouch-shouldered, hands in pockets, impassive. For what seemed like minutes, Dennis was silent and we blamed him, thinking, now you have no answers, like us. But then something animated Dennis's body and he took her hands in his and quieted them.*

Ruth looked at her shoes. Would we like something to nibble on? *she asked, looking up. She hadn't baked in such a long time, since before the cancer came back. No, we said, sweating in the warmth of the house, some of us noticing behind our thoughts the close, medicinal smell of the room. Then, in the backyard, Odie's macaws began to shriek. Ruth laughed.* Well, someone has an appetite, *she said.*

***

If you were one of our sons, you might have scaled Odie's fence at night to blow marijuana smoke at his macaws, told later about opening the birds' cages, watching them careen into the dark and how the next morning, their red yellow blue plumes burned in the bare branches of your own cottonwood, their squawks laying blame. Odie and your father clanging pots and pans beneath the tree to chase the birds home, Odie himself squawking, saying he knew the responsible parties, bugger them. He might then have smiled at you, his sun-mottled face crimping, and you'd imagine him marking your brow for one of the dimpled balls he drove beyond his backyard fence, into the woods where you and your friends sometimes took girls.

***

Odie dotes on these birds, *Ruth said to us on the back porch, as if apologizing. Inside the cage, the macaws stabbed listlessly at the fruit she had sliced. Odie had told us macaws were often drugged and smuggled from South America in spare gas tanks.* Intelligent, rare creatures, *he'd said, some living to be octogenarians, outlasting numerous owners, knowing cruelty and kindness in all forms. They live in the shadow of our house. What might they tell us?*

4

Falling from the tree was easier than climbing it. Through the leaves, Isaac could see the river, a shiny strip of foil. Swallows sliced blue sky. His father had told him flying was kind of falling, too, except more controlled. Last fall, his mother gave him a haircut on the porch and when they cleaned the birdhouse in the spring, they found clumps of his scissored blond hair among the twigs, shredded cigarettes, and Hershey's Kisses wrappers. Once he had stuck feathers from a cat-eaten bird in his hair and his mother had plucked them out, saying birds carried diseases. Mark Soto had a book with photos of a bird-headed dwarf. But that wasn't a bird disease. A little girl with saucer eyes and a big nose. But no real beak, no feathers.

Isaac twisted his torso for a better view of the ground. Two houses over, he saw Mark Soto's older sister Lisa in the little bathroom window, taking a shower. Her hair was sudsy. Lisa taught salsa dancing at Austin High in the afternoons. She looked up at him and waved enthusiastically.

Down below, he heard his mother's voice, shrill, like a birdcall. His father answered her from some other tree. They were like this, apart but together. Like your hands when you danced with someone (not that he wanted to dance with anyone, ever), how they came together and then let go. If you just watched people's hands, they'd tell you a lot, he thought. Where had he heard that? Sometimes his mother's hands shook when she was trying to make him do things. Sometimes his father bit his nails. One time, when he was sleeping over at Mark's house,

Mr. Soto had yelled at Mark for setting off firecrackers in the backyard and Isaac had held Mark's hand in his room. It felt all right. A little weird, but all right. He didn't tell anyone. Earlier that day, they'd taken funny photos in a booth at Amy's Ice Cream that made them look like they had two heads on one body.

He could see his mother's upturned face below, half in shadow. *Expectant*. That was a word she used. But when a woman got pregnant you said she was expect*ing*. Like a pause to think things over. When the baby came out you couldn't send it back.

His mother was calling to him. Her mouth and tongue were up to something. But what? She had been calling to his half-sister, too. He had read a letter that she'd written on the computer. Homer, Alaska, was very far away. He thought of penguins but knew they lived in Antarctica. Things that seemed to go together often didn't—they were just in your head that way. He knew that.

A warm grass smell rose up to meet him. The sun moved through the trees. He heard another voice calling behind his mother's and father's, behind everything. Like an air conditioner that you never noticed humming under your bedroom window until one morning you do. The voice tried to act nice but it wanted something. A wing fluttered by his face. Then he understood: the voice wanted him.

He saw a couple calmly falling beside him. The man's tie whipped behind like a kite tail. The woman's dress billowed. They were holding hands.

The ground was rising. There were two kinds of kites. One was a bird. His father told him once that Leonardo da Vinci remembered, when he was a baby, a kite flicking its tail inside his mouth. Maybe, Isaac's father said, that was why he was so interested in flight. Maybe.

In their bookcase in the den there was an old video of him as a baby, fisting dirt and leaves into his mouth. *No, silly*, his mother said from somewhere. Then she entered the frame, brushed the dirt and leaves away, lifted him up.

5

Behind the soft rasp of cottonwood leaves in his head, P.G. McWhirter could feel his tooth starting to throb again. He was winding through the foothills along the river in a stolen Chevy Blazer, its headlights wandering off into the dripping trees and then settling on the road again. The city across the river shimmered in reds and yellows on the slick pavement. He'd lost his bottle of codeine earlier. Tossed it out the window, more than likely, with the discarded contents of the Lipsy woman's purse. He saw the prescription bottle now, rain-beaded, under some buttery streetlight, among her family photos, lipsticks, and tampons. Soon the pain would begin to spider along his scalp again. His mouth went dry.

He was supposed to drive to a church parking lot on South 1st Street, leave the keys under the mat. He was careful who he worked with, careful what he stole. Older model Suburbans, Blazers, light import trucks. The vehicles were headed to the large industrial cities in Mexico, like Monterrey, where they would blend in. Sometimes he imagined whole Mexican families bunched inside. They'd be coming back from shopping, the hot-ripe smell of oranges and guavas wafting from crates in back. Or sometimes he pictured a group of men sitting on the tailgate in the evening, drinking beer and talking reasonably but passionately about politics or soccer. He'd even begun to write short notes in Spanish to these future owners and tape them inside the glove compartments, complimenting them on their purchase. *What a shame that we shall never meet*, he says in his dictionary Spanish. He felt he had a reputation of sorts for quality. For instance, he wouldn't steal Isuzu trucks because *Consumer Reports*, which he followed, routinely gave them a poor reliability rating.

After dropping off the Blazer, he'd pick up his Civic and head back to his house, where his wife Melinda would be walking the floor with their baby, whose bowels were knotted with colic and whose crying never seemed to stop. Once, he'd given the baby microwaved vanilla ice cream to shut him up, which, admittedly, had made things worse. He could see Melinda rubbing a bare circle on her scalp, like she did. He made her nervous, his ambitions. He had his Allstate office space, his minimal clients, his legitimacy. There was a beauty to it, a symmetry that he ached to explain to her but felt he never could: he would sometimes steal from people he himself insured. His clients received their payouts. The families down in Mexico got their vehicles. And he made a decent living, one that Melinda and the baby shared in, one that, in an economic downturn like this one, he was thankful for. He wondered, though, now as he was driving, if Melinda would leave them again soon, like she had six weeks ago, drop off the baby with a neighbor, just for a few hours, she'd say, until she got her head straight. He thought of the Amarillo Grayhound Station where he and the baby had caught up to her, its peeling stucco exterior, the push broom coming every hour to sweep away his cigarette butts, the baby spitting up the last of the bottled breast milk on his suede jacket, the one he'd found in a Nissan Pathfinder a few days before. He had stared intently at the baby to communicate his displeasure. Weren't they in this together? The baby's eyes still that universal blue, knowing everything and not much. The baby had started screaming. P.G. had gotten looks from the window ticket agents.

Then Melinda had stepped down from the bus and gazed at them through the greenish glass. He'd lifted the baby in the air. Like a trophy? A weapon? He wasn't sure. His wife had a bewildered look on her face. Her shoulders sagged under her purple coat. "Are you a sight for sore eyes," he'd said, hugging her at the door. She'd stiffened. The baby had tugged at her hair. "You're here," was all Melinda had said.

When the girl exploded in the Blazer's high beams, P.G. was sipping from a water bottle to quiet his tooth. She was walking along the creek bridge. Later, he would remember the girl looking back over her shoulder at him, smiling, a funky wide-brimmed hat tilted on her head. *We agreed to meet just here*, she seemed to say. But it would be the photo from the TV news he was actually remembering.

He tried to swerve around her but, instead, went into a slide. The reds and yellows in the road stretched out. Cottonwood leaves roared in his head. His bowels shuddered. Even before he struck the girl and hurled her into the creek bed, he felt all the familiar habits of the world begin to recede.

II

6

After Odie disappeared five months ago, in April, Ruth Dodd had spotted him everywhere. In the frozen food section at the Randall's Supermarket, sitting at the bus stop, lying half-naked in the sun along Auditorium Shores. Winnie knew Ruth was holding a vigil. Who could blame her? Her husband gone without a trace, a reverse miracle, like the stories of people swallowed up by the earth.

For awhile, Ruth's mind seemed swallowed up, too. One weekend Ruth rolled out cookie dough until her palms blistered, delivered ziplock baggies of sugar cookies to neighbors, green-sprinkled with their children's names, most of whom were now grown and gone. At the Pattersons', Ruth strolled into their kitchen, forgetting that her friend Irma Ziesk had moved from there twenty-two years before. And then, six weeks ago, Winnie found Ruth picking tomatoes in the side-yard wearing the Oxford shirt and gray wool slacks Odie wore when he used to make house calls. Winnie called one of Ruth's sisters, and she came down like before to put a stop to the clothes and baking and neighborhood talk. No doctors, no pills, Ruth told the sister. But when Winnie saw Ruth on the porch three weeks later calmly looking over her potted herbs, she was changed. Winnie had to stand on the steps for several seconds before Ruth noticed her. Slow surprise animated her face. Winnie asked how she was, her eyes drawn to Ruth's palms. Ruth said things were as good as possible, considering. She was hopeful, she said. Lately she seemed to be finding objects that she thought she'd lost. For instance, when she got in the car the other morning, she discovered, beside her on the seat, the photo album she'd misplaced weeks ago.

***

Two weeks later, Ruth found Winnie's lost driver's license in her front yard. "I was taking out the trash," Ruth told Winnie, "and there you were in the grass, squinting up at me." This was the day after Dennis and Winnie's Blazer was stolen. Ruth and Winnie sat in Winnie's kitchen. Other items that Ruth had found were laid out on the kitchen table: Winnie's St. David's Pediatric Nurse ID card, two tickets to a Flaming Idiots comedy show, family photos, an expired Gold's Gym card, her diaphragm in its plastic case, and a rain-smeared envelope addressed to her daughter Allison, whom Winnie hadn't seen since she was born. Ruth had used a hair drier on the photos and letter and they curled at their edges like dry leaves. In a ziplock baggie, a prescription bottle for a P.G. McWhirter. Did he live nearby? Was he missing a car? Winnie didn't know, though the name sounded familiar.

Though yesterday the weatherman said that there was only a fifty-percent chance, it had rained all night and was raining still. Water pooled by the backyard fence.

Ruth told Winnie that she'd seen a man skulking behind her own fence last night and suspected it was the same fellow who had stolen Dennis and Winnie's Blazer. Ruth said she'd been afraid to undress. She couldn't sleep. No telling, she said, what was on the man's mind. Winnie told her that it was probably just Darnell Greer back there, working in his woodshop. He makes props for movies, Winnie reminded her. Ruth was quiet. She fingered Winnie's diaphragm case on the table, then realized what she was doing and fumbled it to the floor. "Damn fool thing," she said, reddening, glancing quickly around her feet. Winnie told her it was nothing, that she'd get it later. Ruth's mouth formed a word but passed on it. She coughed. She looked at Winnie, her face emptied, expectant. "So where do you think Darnell is keeping your Blazer?"

7

This is what we imagined the night Odie disappeared: he and Ruth had a fight over the chemotherapy, Odie saying he didn't see the point and Ruth doing what she always did when distressed, driving to the fish market for prawns to saute with a green mango curry, Odie's favorite. On the way home, Ruth would have sat hunched over the wheel of her Plymouth, thinking of her father, who, his brain seized by an aneurysm, had lived with them the last three years of his life. Like Odie, Ruth's father had given away bits of himself. Slivers of his frontal lobe to surgery, fluid to relieve pressure. He'd been a pilot in the early stages of World War II flying cargo planes of supplies to Great Britain but had been too old to fight. In the mid-forties, he had put on a weekly comedy show on a low-powered local radio station in Ft. Worth. A running skit about two rubes from the Panhandle lost in the city, she had told us. Is that you, Leonard? *was his signature line. She remembered also late in his life, after the aneurysm, odd fragments of jokes resurfacing:* I had at one time a large, very fine ape. Did you now, Doctor? Oh yes, a lovely animal. But he grew suddenly ill and, not wanting to lose sight of him altogether, I made his skin into a mat for the table.

We have seen a series of photos in albums and along their living room wall that Odie took of Ruth's father. Every Monday at noon for three years, he posed the old man in the same chair in the same corner of the room. The life-long cock of the old man's head growing ever more pronounced. A sly parting of his lips. Is that you, Leonard? *His right eyelid gradually drooping over a six week period up to where the photos ended.* Good night, *we have thought, seeing the last 3x5 near the bookcase. What was Odie after? Ruth isn't sure, though she knows it has to do with Jonestown, the axis around which his life winds. So she helped Odie position and sometimes cajole her father. In one photo, her disembodied hand clasps her father's shoulder as if he would topple sideways from the frame.*

And driving towards home, it is beneath this photo on the wall that Ruth sees Odie, in the recliner, awake, but dreaming. He and Ruth are standing in an open field at a Ft. Worth airplane stunt show where they met in 1956. Ruth is gazing at the planes overhead, one hand shielding her eyes. She's lovely. He studies the smooth bend of her neck, the slender clavicle bone at its base. He's seized by the desire to percuss her sternum, though he is early in his residency and does not yet know the proper technique. She pulls in her lower lip slightly. He puts his hands in his pockets to hide his erection. She sees him, walks over and takes his arm, speaks close to his ear because of the drone of the planes, so close he can feel her breath and smell rose talcum on her skin. She says she's pregnant, though he knows her brief pregnancy and this event—their first meeting—are years apart. Ruth lets go of Odie's arm, bends at the waist near a water fountain, and vomits. Then she is ponderously heavy and back-bowed, her breasts full. By the time she waddles to the bleachers, her water breaks, gushing over Odie's feet like a great tide, sweeping his slippers from him. He is down on all fours looking for the goddamn things when she shouts at him. Odie looks up to see her mouth form a perfect circle, just as a stunt plane falters in its loop and noses into the field.

Odie crawled from the recliner and left the house in his bare feet. Nothing, other than Odie, was missing or out of place.

***

If you lived a street over, and happened to take your trash to the curb that evening, you might have seen flashlights flaring off trees along Johnson Creek, where we poked through the brush, looking for Odie. Instead we found refuse swept here by past floods: A child's mangled bike, mateless shoes, a large painted sign that welcomed baseball fans. Then, further in, beneath a limestone overhang, a dark bundle of sleeping bag we at first took for a man. A few of us lifted its saggy weight with sticks. Flattened on the smooth limestone ledge, a collection of bras and panties. We laughed nervously, some imagining awkward encounters in woods like these, the frantic peeling away of clothes, another's pale, taut skin against our own.

We slept fitfully. The macaws startled Dennis awake with cries like small children's. Winnie dreamed her long-dead parents were approaching the coast inside a giant sea snail. Neogastropoda. *A name she told Dennis later she couldn't get out of her head.*

An article appeared in the next morning's paper with a photo of Odie. Sunfreckled. Gaptoothed. Missing.

Dogs give them away. Our sons' feet scuffle beneath Winnie's lit window, where, through the curtains, they'd seen a scrap of breast. Some nights, we call out from our porches, threaten them with beatings. But before we can catch and wring them like wet towels, they are off across lawns and between the pine bones of the new duplexes we have for ten years fought off. We hear them scrape over the fence beyond the lots where they once built tree forts with stolen lumber. They are headed for the river, its fractured rise of train trestle, where they drink beer and climb the creosote rafters above the dark water, mocking us with the miraculous rise of their bodies.

* * *

Tonkawa Indians once raised their children along our river, not far from Red Bud Island where Dennis takes Isaac fishing. Periodic floods washed over the banks then, even as they do now, carrying sediment, uprooting trees, unearthing the remains of their dead. But the Tonkawa always moved back, even occupying the same limestone shelters where their flood-lost children once played, as if they could not help themselves. And when the Tonkawa ate their captured Comanche enemies, as they often did, pregnant women were given the largest portions. Courage and strength. That is what they hoped to swallow.

8

In the cool of the evening, Odie and Jim Jones walk along the riverbank. Odie is barefoot.

Words fail, Jones says.

That's it? Words fail?

I'd place my hands on their shoulders, look at them with great sympathy—that was the hard part, you understand—then I'd say it. It was sincere. I couldn't think of anything else. I was shooting blanks.

They left you.

Not many, Odie. You'd be surprised.

They were afraid.

They sought rapture.

I think about it, the jungle.

'It has a fascination, too, that goes to work upon him.' That's Conrad.

You asked me to come. On that day.

Coincidence. I forgot you were coming. Where the hell are your shoes, anyway?

You waited.

Christalmighty. Details. It was a busy time.

The cicadas were singing.

An axis around which your life winds. That's what they say, Odie.

Who says that?

Everyone.

You were in the kitchen when I found you, eating a melon.

The moment of the soul's attentiveness. Like Christ in the garden. Waiting.

For what?

For what God had to say. For the gun barrel at the back of my skull.

You were spitting melon seeds onto the floor.

The end, when it comes, is a small thing, a stick in the river—but it parts the water, alters its course, all the same. Otherwise the goddamn thing flows on. Tick without tock is nothing.

It was said you were dying. That you mistook your dying for theirs.

Words fail, Odie.

Yes, they do.

9

P.G. told himself it was a deer. The rain-smeared road. Light and shadow. He was sitting in the Chevy Blazer, halfway down the embankment. The engine was still running. He pulled the Blazer further into the trees, turned off the headlights, got out. It was raining harder. On the hill above, the gauzy lights of houses. Below was the creek. He could hear rushing water. The pain crept from his tooth to his scalp, spidery and alive. He remembered, when he was a kid, sneaking back to his parents' bedroom with his brothers to stick his finger behind the radio for a shock. Lips tingling. The gleaming white medicine cabinet in the bathroom.

He took a swallow from the water bottle, held it in his mouth until the pain drained away. His legs were weak. He pointed the flashlight he'd found in the glove box toward the rushing creek below. A tire, a Century 21 Realty sign, then, near a fence post, a red dress, the girl. One knee drawn up, an arm thrown behind her head, as if she was just waking up some lazy Saturday. She was missing a shoe.

Further down the creek, he saw an old man in a bathrobe leaning against a tree.

10

In the early morning, if you jogged along the greenbelt at the base of our hill, you would glimpse patches of river through the cypress and cottonwood, and when you neared its bend where the trees give way, see scullers glide past, their ebb and flow cutting a thin ripple in the glassy water behind. Eventually they circle Red Bud Island, where along the shore, Isaac tires of rebaiting his hook with minnows and skips rocks instead, saying the river smells like a wet dog. Beside him, Dennis points downriver to where a rock outcropping had once formed the deep eddy for which the neighborhood was named. He tells Isaac how they dynamited it long ago because dozens of people drowned there in the 1920s. I wouldn't have, *Isaac tells him.* I would've held my breath. *Isaac's eyes narrow and he sucks air, staring at the distant space in the river.*

Once, while they were fishing, a man had called them over to see what was on his trotline. He pulled from the water a three-foot alligator gar, its head narrowed into a long snout. Otherworldly. Early Pleistocene, *the man said,* a damn antique. *The gar slapped its slender body against the tree and the man gripped its snout and tail, firm. Held it out for Isaac.* Go ahead, *the man had said.* Touch him. Some history there. *When Isaac touched the clamped-shut teeth, he smiled sheepishly up at the man, and something sank in Dennis's stomach. The man let Isaac pick out a lure from his tackle box to keep.*

Back before he disappeared, Dennis had seen Odie a few times along Johnson Creek, poking at rocky crevices with a hand spade, looking for awls, arrowheads, and the like. But there were other artifacts that Odie was partial to as well: rusted Sucret boxes, television tubes, chrome knobs, watches, license plates. He kept an ancient yellowed pair of dentures wrapped in foil at home. Odie had once held the dentures up, making for them a mouth with his hand. Had a tongue in it and could sing once, *he'd said to Dennis and laughed until tears rose in his eyes.*

We know some things about Winnie: when she was nineteen, she had lived with her instructor, a marine biologist at Texas A&M, Galveston. She said she loved his sense of humor, and, of course, the sex, both of which had faded when, in the early 1980s, they had spent nearly a year on the Mexican Baja, where he researched large sea mollusks. Winnie, tanned, in a wide-brimmed hat and red bikini top, stares out from the pages of a scrapbook we've seen. She's smiling but turned sideways, a hand holding the crown of her hat, as though reluctant to pose. Doubtful. This will not last, the gesture seems to say, as if she'd just conjured an image of the biologist's collection of unshelled mollusks floating in jars of formaldehyde in their extra bedroom. Only a few days after this photo was taken, she would find out she was pregnant. And her thinking the nausea was a reaction to shellfish. When she had decided to have the baby, the marine biologist tried to hide his disappointment by throwing himself into books on prenatal care and natural childbirth. But his mood swung wildly. Once she found him naked on the kitchen floor wrapped in ice water-soaked bath towels. It's an Icelandic cure, *he'd told her.* For what? Pregnancy? *she'd asked. And when she told him about the adoption, he'd fingered an embryology book—relieved, she knew—and asked,* are you sure? *in a voice that believed itself. At the hospital, he held her hand while she asked for the epidural. She did not look at him. She thought of a conch shell, hard, impervious. Afterwards, she did not want to hold her daughter, but her body demanded it. Her bones ached is what she would tell Ruth later.*

And now, nineteen years later, she confessed to Ruth she sometimes caught herself absurdly scanning crowds at college football games on TV, or looking up suddenly while cooking dinner, drawn to a female voice on the evening news. For a time, she had even subscribed to a college fashion magazine and cut out models with hazel eyes, curly hair, and, she imagined, a subtle intelligence and sense of style.

***

The marine biologist tried to kill himself. Dennis had told us this at a party once. After Winnie left him for the third and final time and had started dating Dennis, the biologist began calling at all hours. We all need to talk, the biologist said. There were threats, mostly about what he would do to himself, Dennis had said. Winnie had spoken gently to him, asked about his medication. Dennis had imagined him pickled in one of his jars. Finally, Winnie had moved in with Dennis and the calls had stopped. Then, one day, the biologist came by the law offices where Dennis was clerking part-time, and by chance Dennis wasn't at his desk. Instead, he and the biologist had stood one urinal apart in the office men's room, Dennis recognizing him from pictures he'd seen. But the biologist, knowing nothing more than Dennis's name, had stared at the shiny tiles, oblivious, a frayed look to his bearded face. He seemed someplace else. For a while afterward, Dennis felt weirdly exhilarated. But the biologist's expression had stayed with him. Dennis wondered if the biologist might be coming to an important decision about himself, something irrevocable. And when Dennis and Winnie were in Chicago a month later, Dennis kept thinking the biologist would pop out of a doorway or alley, although he knew he was thousands of miles away. And when they got lost coming back from Greek Town late one night, and crossed a metal draw bridge that spanned the Chicago River, it occurred to him that he had not seen anyone else walking. That he'd gotten them lost. A few cars slipped by quickly, their tires ringing on the metal of the bridge. Below, he heard water lapping at the concrete sides of the canal. Winnie was tugging his shoulder, saying you lost bastard, in the giggly half-serious way she does right before she actually gets quiet and pissed. Then behind them, someone said they were some lucky motherfuckers because Saturday night was lotto night, otherwise he wouldn't be out. Dennis had glanced back quickly, seized by the image of the biologist's stricken face. A bearded black man stared back. What ya'll doing here? Should be home letting this man get into your sweetbreads. *Dennis told Winnie not to turn around, only to keep walking. Winnie beside him, stiff, her eyes glancing down a cross street, thinking a cab, maybe a cab. And then a few seconds later, a cab did pass swiftly by, and inside, Dennis could see moon-like faces lit up for a moment by a streetlight, then nothing. His stomach tumbled. Now two sets of footsteps behind. They walked on, faster. Someone kicked his heels and he stumbled slightly.* Whoo, I smell something, *a second voice said behind and laughed. Then a hand slapped Dennis's ear. Ringing. He felt the ear with his fingers, looked at Winnie, wild-eyed, her face drawn. He wanted to tell her not to worry.* Stay the fuck back, Nathan, *the first voice said,* these people with me. *Feet scuffled. Dennis said he turned to see the two black men pressed against one another. And it struck Dennis suddenly that he and Winnie would be shot. They would bleed to death here simply because he had taken a wrong turn. He turned back, kept walking. Beside him, he heard Winnie say his name.*

At the party, this is where Dennis had paused, and then said it was a close call, that the second man had slunk off and the bearded man had taken them a quarter-mile to the elevated train, and then in front of the turnstiles, asked them for a twenty for the Lotto. If I win, we'll split it, *he'd said.*

We imagined something else: Dennis and Winnie at the curb. The men behind. A few blocks away, a blue sign that said Dixie Cream Donuts. A light on inside where the baker was working. One-hundred yards. Run. *The thought out before Dennis can stifle it. But we know this is our own weakness we are seeing and it settles like a stone in the belly.*

Anyway, Dennis had said at the party, when he and Winnie got back to the hotel, there was a message from a mutual friend that the biologist had shot himself.

11

In the pediatric break room, Prakosh, one of the radiologists, was telling Winnie a story. The TV news was on. Prakosh was from Bangladesh and was often astonished by the grave tone of the American news broadcasters. "You people and your tragedies," he'd say. "We would throw a party if such things happened to us." He once told her how, in 1991, a series of typhoon waves killed more than 130,000 Bangladeshis. He dumped his box of Junior Mints on the table, touched their chocolate heads. "And do they each have a special plaque? No, they do not." Prakosh's hair was thinning on top and Winnie had thought absently of placing her hand there to feel his voice resonate through his skull. He sometimes asked her out for drinks after their common shifts, a kind of running joke that wasn't a joke, she knew. When she said no, he would say that it was a tragedy.

The story Prakosh was telling Winnie now was about a baby he'd seen several years ago who could not stop crying. "He only stopped to eat and defecate," Prakosh said.

"Not so different from us," Winnie said.

"You are right. Not so different." Prakosh smiled. He said that a week after the boy's parents took him home, they called the doctor, saying that the boy was still crying, what should they do? The parents were delirious without sleep. The doctor told them it was most likely an acid reflux, nothing to worry about. But they were worried. These people had lived in rural Mexico before immigrating. They believed in the unseen. What had happened before the child entered the world to make him so angry with them? "This is, of course, the thing," Prakosh said. He got up and scanned the vending machine selections. "We pass between two darknesses. Those who might inform us about either end—newborns and the dead—cannot do so."

Prakosh settled back in his chair. "Would you share my Skittles?" he said. "Or is this perhaps too intimate?"

Winnie smiled and said she already felt compromised by the romantic setting.

Prakosh went on: As if to prove a point, the boy stopped eating. The parents took him back to the hospital for CAT scans and tests, where Prakosh found a dark lump: a tumor in his abdominal cavity. After three weeks on an IV, as soon as the boy was strong enough, the doctors went in to remove the mass. But what they discovered instead, attached to an artery along his abdominal wall, was the boy's brother, the size of a kiwi. The cell division had gone wrong somehow, the doctor explained later. The boy had enveloped his brother. Or the brother had invaded the boy. It depended on how one looked at it, Prakosh said. In any case, removing the brother was difficult because of the artery. Touch and go. Needless to say, nothing could be done for the brother. The boy had gotten most of the nutrients from the mother. The brother was undeveloped, his skin translucent. You could see tiny organs inside.

Prakosh said the boy's grandmother in Mexico heard it all through translation and thought that the boy had somehow eaten his brother. The boy's mother had a breakdown.

Prakosh cupped a handful of Skittles to his mouth.

Winnie saw, not the brother, but her own daughter as she was many months before Winnie gave birth: a pale, sightless, creature groping her way along the sea floor. Alone as only God is alone.

Prakosh narrowed his eyes at her across the table. “So the boy was found and the brother lost. Is the story a miracle that one prays for? Or a tragedy that one prays against?”

Winnie didn’t know.

12

Every few weeks, Dennis drives out near Dripping Springs to visit Sonny Farbrother. Sonny had hired Dennis months ago to fend off a guardianship case Sonny's daughter had filed. She wanted to move Sonny to a care facility in Oklahoma where she lived. Sonny called it the necropolis. He said he was fine despite his advanced emphysema, the junk piled in the kitchen, despite the problem with the rats. Dennis told him his daughter only wanted to help, that Sonny might want to reconsider. But Sonny wouldn't even talk to her. "I'll tell you what she's after," Sonny said, and pretended to cup something lightly in his palm, then squeeze it shut. "My balls." Dennis noticed how slender and feminine the hands were, as if they'd somehow been kept apart from the withered rest of him.

Sonny had once owned an import shop off Highway 290, where Dennis worked the summer he turned fifteen. Some nights, after Dennis totaled out the register, Sonny would grab a six-pack from the fridge, and sit with Dennis on the loading bay steps behind the shop and tell him stories while they drank beer.

Sonny had been a Hollywood movie Indian in the 1950s but claimed to be a real Indian, a Tonkawa. He said he'd grown up on a reservation in Oklahoma and trained as a Golden Gloves boxer before going out to LA and getting his break in the movies. His daughter, Margo, was still on the reservation and was planning to visit him at Christmas, he'd said. But some people, including Dennis's Uncle Tap, said Sonny wasn't Indian at all but Mexican and that he'd been in and out of jail, though no one could say for what.

Sonny had once shown Dennis a black and white photo of himself and John Wayne in swimsuits beside a hotel swimming pool, beer bottles in their hands. Ropes of muscle ran along Sonny's dark arms in the picture and Dennis thought he looked like a boxer. Confident and dangerous, not dried up the way he looked now. Wayne, his blurred hand gesturing with a cigarette, had his mouth open in the middle of a sentence. "Duke hated horses," Sonny told Dennis, as if explaining the difference between Wayne and himself. Sonny told him about living on location in Guanajuato, Mexico, and in Monument Valley, where they filmed *The Searchers*. "Every day, I got killed," Sonny said. "Stabbed. Shot. Thrown off my horse. Some goddamn acting." He clinked Dennis's bottle with his own, making Dennis feel awkward but a part of Sonny's story just the same. Out in Hollywood, Sonny said, he lived out of hotels, slept with dozens of strange and beautiful women, making some insanely jealous. An image rose in Dennis's head of naked women cartwheeling behind Sonny and John Wayne, their skin smooth and white except for the dark wedges between their legs, their bodies pinwheeling slowly into the glistening pool.

Sonny told Dennis that one of the women, a make-up artist, had tried to kill him. "She gave me an extra mouth," Sonny said, lifting up his shirt, revealing in the porch light a half-dollar size gouge in his belly, the skin puckered at its edges. "Put your finger in there and it won't come back," he said, grinning obscenely. Dennis looked off at car headlights passing on the highway to have somewhere else to look. He swallowed hard on his beer. Sonny explained how just after a particularly bad fight—one in which they'd drunkenly said and done unpardonable things to one another and then smashed lamps, room service dishes, and overturned the TV—the make-up artist had stepped into the bathroom where he was peeing, holding a jagged crescent of broken dish in her hand. She was naked, her neck and chest flushed, eyes wide. Radiant. "What are you planning to do with that?" he'd asked her. He'd laughed weakly when he'd said it: a short chuckle that caught in his throat. He kept peeing. He'd even had time to sidestep her when she'd lunged at him, but for some reason—maybe the vodka—he hadn't moved. She stuck the crescent of dish just under his ribs. It hung out of him at an odd angle, as if finding a pocket. But he felt nothing, no pain. Maybe, he'd thought absurdly, he had mimicked pain for so long in movies that he'd become immune to it. The make-up artist's hand, a beautiful slender thing, alternately moved between the crescent and his face. Caressing. Oh how she loved him.

"She was crazy," Dennis said. He glanced at the spot where the mouth had appeared beneath Sonny's shirt, then looked down at his own boots.

Sonny said that the next thing he knew, he was staring up at his make-up artist from the bathroom floor and that beyond her face were the watermarks on the ceiling. Pain coiled through him now. White wall tiles gleamed. He pulled the crescent free from its pocket, partly because it seemed the source of the pain, which clouded everything, and partly because he thought this way the make-up artist would stop fretting and apologizing which annoyed him to no end. Blood went everywhere. After awhile, he grew cold. She wrapped him in the bedsheet there on the tiled floor, even swathing his head turban-like with a towel. Sonny lay there, he said, for what seemed like hours, slowly bleeding to death. "Sonny, you don't look so good," his make-up artist said at one point. She sang a Nat King Cole song to him, her bleach blonde head resting on his chest, her voice vibrating against his sternum. She had a beautiful alto, he said. He passed in and out of consciousness. He woke to find her brushing something onto his face. Beside her on the tile, her make-up kit stood open. "I'm putting some color back in your cheeks," she said. "Hold still." She'd held the mirror up for him to see. The image? A painted warrior. On his head, a headdress made from a large white crane. Its eyes shone sky blue. His make-up artist ran her fingers through its plumes singing his name. "This is what I saw, no lie," Sonny said. "It was a vision."

"A vision?"

"The crane is my guardian spirit."

"Oh."

"I tried to have a headdress made just like it, but cranes are endangered." Sonny flicked his cigarette into the gravel and spat. "Well, the room service guy came by to pick up the lunch dishes and when he heard the singing he mistook it for somebody inviting him in. Pure luck. Another thirty minutes and I'd have bought it." Sonny drank from his beer, then tapped another cigarette from a pack. He said he supposed what he and the make-up artist felt for one another was a kind of love, if looked at a certain way. That violence and rage were a part of love, too. "I read a story once about how the first human being was cut in halves, male and female, and how those separate halves had looked for each other, far and wide. When they finally found one another, though, and tried to come together, too many connecting pieces had broken off. So now, they spite one another for being what they can't help being," Sonny said.

"What happened to the girl?" Dennis asked.

"Oh. I ended up marrying her," Sonny had laughed.

III

13

Under the expressway bridge, Odie sits beside Jones, picking through a plastic garbage bag full of clothes.

It's getting much colder at night, Odie says, lifting a wool sweater into the weak amber of the streetlight. Hypothermia can creep up on you.

There's nothing to death, Jones says.

Easy for you to say. You're dead.

It's just walking one room to another.

Then why didn't you—

Don't give me that, Odie. You of all goddamn people.

You hesitated.

Hesitated? Without me, life had no meaning. I was the best thing they'd ever seen.

Well, the last thing anyway.

I was a damn fine-looking man, Odie.

You colored your hair.

Women do love cunnilingus.

The gun was on the floor, Odie says.

Flies to honey. I remember this one who liked to—

You're not listening.

I am. It's just that the memories are heady things, like ripe mangoes. Jones pats the back of his own head, thoughtfully. Grins.

Stop that, Odie says.

What?

The thing with your head.

What? This? Jones does it again. The art of memory, he says, was born in calamity.

How portentous, Odie says.

Jesus, what a grump. Anyway, this old Greek fella, Simonides, invented memory.

Like Ben Franklin invented electricity?

Semantics, Odie. This Simonides was giving a great oration at a banquet hall. Back in antiquity, they were always paying tribute to this goddamn person or the other. So, Simonides was singing his host's praises when midway through someone rings the doorbell and wants to speak with him. Two beautiful young men, the doorman says. Eyebrows raise. Well, Simonides, the fudge-packer that he is, steps outside. Nobody there. Just then, the banquet hall collapses and everyone is crushed beyond recognition. The gods' retribution, etc. The grieving families, though, are left with a jumble of parts. But, because of his memory, Simonides knows where each guest was sitting. He's able to piece old Xeres and the gang back together again. But the thing is, all they had was Simonides's word. How do they know he's right? He's probably got survivor's guilt. Wants to make amends. What if, in the end, it's not really Xeres's arm and leg?

Odie looks at Jones. You were eating a melon, casual-like, he says. The stench all around. I picked up the gun off the floor. I weighed it in my hand.

I never liked firearms, Jones says, waving Odie off. They do change people so.

14

When Dennis left Winnie and the other mourners in the den and headed down the darkened hall to the bathroom, he saw Natalie's closed bedroom door. A strip of light beneath. He nearly walked past but, instead, found his hand on the knob. He could hear a low humming inside. He glanced down the hall. No one. He turned the knob, stepped inside. An aquarium glowed pale green in the corner. Inside, brilliant yellow fish swam around a conch shell. He wondered if anyone had remembered to feed them. The air felt moist. On the walls, framed movie stills from *Giant* and *The Last Picture Show*. French movie posters. On the desk were books. *One Hundred Years of Solitude, Astonish Yourself! Experiments in the Philosophy of Everyday Life*. Her laptop computer sat open. Inside it were emails he'd sent her. He would have to delete them, he supposed. Her hat hung on the bedpost. He sat on the bed and held the hat in his lap. A portion of the brim was frayed, where, he imagined, it had rubbed the back of her lifeguard chair.

Someone was headed down the hall. He got up, hid himself in the closet among her hanging clothes. Smells of lotion, chlorine, something vaguely sweet. She was almost there in the pleats and cuffs. Sometimes, he remembered, she brought Swedish fish candies for the kids at the pool. They'd do tricks for her. Underwater flips. Hold their breath while sitting on the pool bottom. She'd tell stories of the time her father took her camping in Big Bend—right after he'd lost her in a custody battle, Dennis knew—and had stayed gone two weeks. They'd had to live off the land, she'd said. She had skinned jackrabbits with a penknife, stole scrub jay eggs from nests. A steady gaze from her made the children terrified and bold, just as it had him.

When the bedroom door opened, the thick smell of flowers drifted in from the den. Low voices. His wife's from down the hall. *I remember*, she was saying. Then the bedroom door closed. What was Winnie remembering? It seemed important that he know. He watched through the slats of the closet door as Natalie's mother replaced the hat on the bedpost, then walked in circles around the room, her hands clasped behind her head like a prisoner.

15

We knew about Winnie's letters to her daughter. Keep this under your hat, *we'd say to one another, but words have a life of their own. Her dreams, too, washed down our streets with the flood waters, eddied around xeriscaped medians, pooled in low-lying backyards. And so, in this way, her dream bled into our own and fixed before our eyes: Winnie is back in Chicago. It's night and she and Dennis are walking. On either side of Division Street, the tenement buildings are dark but they can see small fires flickering on some of the floors. Newspaper and debris cling to a chain-link fence that is bent like a breaking wave. Winnie is telling Dennis that her lost daughter Allison is on a fishing boat in Alaska. The detective who has helped find her through tax records and credit reports reminds her of Dennis, with his funny avoidance of conflicts. Whenever Dennis disagreed with her, he'd clear his throat and say,* I guess that's one way to look at it. *It got on her nerves. His passivity.* Guess that's one way to look at putting your eye out. *Dennis winces beside her and his eye is gone.* Jesus, Winnie, *he says. She's seized by regret. She loves Dennis. Even during the silences in their lovemaking or when he looks at Natalie Branch in that way, or at this moment, when she sees panic in his one good eye as the two men come up from behind.* What y'all doing here? *She loves Dennis. He is not lost. She wants to have another baby with him, though she knows at 39 she shouldn't. She wants to cut his hair on their porch and tease him about his gray. She gently puts his eye back, strokes his cheek with her small-boned hand.*

The wind picks up. It begins to rain. Whitecaps form out on Lake Michigan, then quickly become 25-foot swells. She knows it's not Lake Michigan at all, but Alaska. The storm was headed north toward Anchorage and then changed directions. Still, the captain thought the fishing boat could outrun it. It caught them forty miles off Kodiak Island. From shore, Winnie sees the boat's lights disappear from the horizon as it hits a trough. Inside, Allison is asleep in her bunk one minute, tossed in the air the next. She gashes the bridge of her nose on the bed above. The coppery taste of blood in her mouth. She shouts but can't hear herself above the caterwaul from the galley, as stove, fridge, microwave, wrench themselves from bolts and wall. Her head is thudding. Zach, her boyfriend, was supposed to wake her up before the storm hit. The boat falls into another trough and her stomach lurches. Lights flicker. She pulls on her boots and staggers into the galley, walls and floor pitching. Food from the fridge is strewn in red and brown islands over the galley floor. She climbs the ladder up to the wheelhouse, where the crew is huddled together, passing a joint. A few faces look up blankly as if they can't quite place her. Zach is staring out the window. Teddy Box says in a mildly interested voice that her nose is bleeding. Everyone sticks to the obvious, tells jokes. At the window, every twenty seconds or so, Zach shouts out a wave, and Terrence, the captain, steers toward it. Here's one! There's another! *Then, after awhile, the waves seem to rise in all directions and other crewmembers join in, pointing, yelling. Allison eyes the inflatable hypothermia suits squatting in the corner. Teddy Box says, all things considered, he's dropping some acid. He starts to sing a Roy Orbison song in a falsetto.* I was all right, for a while. *Then he grows quiet.*

***

We know some things about Allison: She and Zach had come to Alaska a year ago from Houston. Zach had a friend in Homer who would set them up in the fish canneries. They'd live in tents out on the Spit in the summer. Later, they planned to find jobs with the forest service, save their money and buy a small place in Anchorage, catch and smoke their own salmon. But after the first few weeks of gutting fish in the frigid canneries, the briny stink seemed to follow them everywhere. Zach would flush his nose with saline, convinced the smell had settled in the membranes. Allison plucked fish entrails from her hair. Then six months later, their luck turned and they'd gotten deckhand jobs on a fishing boat, the Quintessence, *earning a small percentage of the catch. An internship, the skipper had called it. They took turns baiting the fish pots, cooking, clearing the ship's bilge. When pulling in fish, they'd slice their hands on the lines. They smeared on ointment used for chapped cow udders to keep the cuts from going septic and wore socks as mittens while they slept. The first week out, she and Zach had made love on his bunk with the socks on, and Allison had felt like a clumsy astronaut, solitary and forlorn.*

Seven weeks later, after a missed period and a bout of vomiting, she found she was pregnant.

***

Beside Allison in the wheelhouse, Teddy Box says that he'd had a dream a few nights ago that all the cod he'd ever gaffed were swimming around inside him. He'd felt them poking at his organs, trying to find a way out. Someone tells Teddy to shut the fuck up.

Zach is still busy pointing out waves. His face is up next to the glass. Every so often he wipes away his own breath to see. She hasn't told him about the baby, though she's not sure why. She can smell the charged air around them, the minerals in the waves, and it strikes her that these are the smells of indifference, that the next wave will hit them sideways, crash through the wheelhouse window. A roaring in her ears like her own blood, then nothing.

As if on cue, a wave appears in the wheelhouse window. It rises high above the bow, gray and impalpable in the floodlights. Someone makes a low animal sound. It will pass through us, *Allison thinks, as if she is part of our dream. The boat shudders and pitches her to the floor. Lights flicker out. She can see a joint glowing faintly between someone's fingers. No one says anything. The ship groans. It seems to her that what the world wants, above all else, is to come apart. Each wave a promise of this. Recognizing something of itself in you. But she refuses them like suitors.* Pass through us, *she says again and again, and, as if by some magic, each wave does. And after midnight sometime, they find an island cove. They wait out the storm through the night.*

When they return to port in Homer *the next day, they find everyone has given them up for dead. A sure-as-shit miracle, people say. 25 foot swells. We imagine them welcomed in bars as ghosts or saints. Taped by a cash register, a photo of a smiling Teddy Box in an orange hypothermia suit, bobbing in the cove.*

Months later, in town, Allison, her belly rounded and tight, is sought after to bless children.

16

Every few seconds the girl's fingers fluttered and her eyes darted around under their lids, like she was dreaming. Her head was turned in a funny way that made P.G. want to look at her bare foot. Her toenails were painted silver. A Band-Aid clung to her heel.

P.G. sipped from the water bottle to quiet his tooth.

Rain raked the stony ground.

Things in her were broken, he was sure. But if he could get her out of the creekbed, those things could be mended. He was afraid to carry her because of her head. Afraid, too, of everything that would follow. Gently, gently, he told himself. The old man near the tree could help, he thought. P.G. called out to him, pointed the flashlight where the old man had been standing, fifteen feet away. The old man stared back. His bathrobe, muddied, tattered. P.G. could see there was a hole in his throat.

The girl murmured something.

The creek was rising.

P.G. tried to explain to the old man that it wasn't his fault, that the girl came out of nowhere.

The girl sighed deeply.

"I think something's wrong with her neck," P.G. called out, as if he expected the old man to tell him it wasn't so.

The old man came within a few feet, said in a rasp, "I saw headlights coming down the hill. I knew who it would be."

"Right," P.G. said. Crazy as a shit house rat, he thought.

And here he was looking to the old man for help. He felt his legs weaken a little, failure begin to settle in.

He squatted down again beside the girl, checked her breathing. He thought he could feel warmth against his cheek. Her dress was ripped along the shoulder where she had hit the ground, he supposed. His stomach flopped. He decided not to look too closely anymore and only focus on the red dress. An older style. Little roses everywhere. Where had she been tonight? A party? Kissing her boyfriend afterwards in his car. The boyfriend's unsteady hand cupping her breast. Her fevered skin. The pulse beneath, thrum, thrum, thrum, like a promise.

He could feel the old man's eyes on him.

It was raining harder. A song played somewhere: Dwight Yoakum sang "Turn It On, Turn it Up, Turn Me Loose." He had left the radio on in the Blazer.

The girl murmured again. He put the flashlight down and bent low so he could hear. Stroked her forehead the way he did his son's when he ran a fever. Smoothed her bangs. Then she was quiet and still. He sat there for several minutes, holding her hand. She was sleeping, he told himself.

The creek was rushing out of its banks. His shoes, filling with water.

He looked for his water bottle but couldn't find it. The old man, too, was gone. He put the flashlight in his back pants pocket. Tried to lift the girl, a hand supporting her head. Gently, he cautioned himself. Then there was a roaring sound and the ground gave way under him and he was swept forward, losing hold of her. He went under. Scraped over rocks, roots. He clung to a branch and pulled himself to the side. Grabbed the flashlight from his pocket, swept the creek with it, looking for the girl. He scrambled up the bank, began to run, stumbled, pants legs catching on thorns. The flashlight beam jittered in the trees. He spotted the girl for a moment downstream but lost her. Then, through a gap in the trees, the flashlight shone on her pale foot, her body slowed by a gnarled cypress root. He set his feet along the muddied bank, bent at the knees, and leaped as if his legs still held their spring.

17

Some nights the macaws cried like babies. It was a lonely sound. They missed Mr. Dodd, Isaac's father said. It seemed to Isaac that they missed Natalie, too. That they went on missing things and couldn't stop. To them, the houses and trees and people looked, from the air, like the features of a familiar face. The way his mother's face looked, squinting up at him in the tree. But on the ground, nothing fit together. After he fell, he decided he wouldn't look at his arm. He would watch his mother's face and she would tell him how to feel. Angry and afraid were the first things. Then her face loosened into something that scared him more because it was further away. "Careful or they'll separate you from your digits," Mr. Dodd croaked once when Isaac hooked his fingers through the macaw's wire cage. Digits were fingers. He knew that. But the macaws wouldn't eat them. Not really. Mr. Dodd was teasing. Like when he pretended to tear your five dollar bill in half or pulled coins from your ears. Pence was what he called pennies because Mr. Dodd was born in England. For a pence, he said, you could buy enough sweets to rot your teeth. When Isaac broke his arm, the doctors had put three metal pins inside his elbow. *Pence* and *pins* sounded alike but were different. His father said there were things at work inside people that would surprise you. Isaac's Great Aunt Virgie had a pacemaker that kept her heart from falling asleep. Like an elbow nudge to wake it up. She had diabetes and wasn't supposed to eat sweets but sometimes did. His Great Uncle Tap one time found a half-eaten Heath Bar in the toe of her dress shoe. The macaws' sweets were nuts and fruit. They didn't have teeth. The bottom of their cage was covered in eaten-out pecan shells and black orange rinds.

Mr. Dodd told him that the macaws were really a cheeky boy and girl he'd known in Guyana. Their parents had been good, loving parents, but when their mother died (she had eaten a spoiled mango, Mr. Dodd said), the father grieved so much that he began to forget them. He'd forget to walk them home from school in the afternoon or to cook them prawns for supper. So the boy and the girl, being cheeky, sprouted feathers and made terrible squawking sounds to get their father's attention. But the father's memory of them faded even as their plumes grew more brilliant. After a time, Mr. Dodd said in his croaking voice, their father grew so annoyed at their racket that whenever they appeared, he tossed stones at them. So they climbed higher and higher into the tree branches, listening and watching below for signs of their father. Mr. Dodd said that instead of food, the boy and girl fed on memories of their life before. They knew that the only way they could become human again was to eat the flesh of another child.

Isaac looked at Mr. Dodd and grinned because that's what you did. Mr. Dodd was teasing. He offered Isaac a pistachio, then flicked one into the macaws' cage. On their broomstick perch, the macaws shifted their feet.

***

One night, not long after Isaac broke his arm, he dreamed Mr. Dodd crept through his bedroom window, cut open his cast and inside were his withered-up stick arm and three shiny pennies. Mr. Dodd shook the cast and the pennies rattled out into his hand.

* * *

The week before Christmas, Isaac went with his father to deliver smoked hams to some of his father's clients. It had turned colder and Isaac could smell wood smoke from the fireplaces. In a neighborhood off South 1st Street, near the State School for the Deaf, they visited a deaf woman named Sara who wrote down everything on a pad of paper instead of talking. She wrote very fast and made a *whisk-whisk* sound with the pencil as she went. On the wall near the back door was a photo of a freckled man in a soldier's uniform. Isaac wondered if the man was still a soldier and if he wrote her letters from somewhere far away. He liked how letters sometimes smelled like the people who wrote them. How long would the smell last? he wondered. The woman slid the pad to his father across the kitchen table and his father wrote back. One time, his father looked down at the notepad and laughed. It seemed loud in the kitchen after all the writing. Isaac realized that he hadn't heard his father laugh in a long time. The woman laughed too. Hers was a funny, warbling sound like a bird, even though she had never heard one. Isaac joined in, even though he didn't know why it had started.

Later, his father pulled into the dry cleaners that Mr. Branch, Natalie's father, owned. Mr. Branch needed to sign some legal papers, his father said. Make changes to his will. *Survivorship* meant that you outlived someone. His father had told him that. Isaac's mother had told him how, when he was two, Isaac had choked on a cherry tomato half his father had given him. His face had turned blue. His father stuck his finger down Isaac's throat and plucked it out. And even though Isaac couldn't remember any of it, he sometimes pretended he could. Sometimes his father saved him and sometimes he didn't. If you had *survivorship*, you could think about being dead, but if you didn't, you couldn't think at all. What happened to your left-behind things when you died? Isaac didn't know. He wondered about the silver ankle bracelet he'd seen his father buy for Natalie at the jewelry place. "Just a little something for mom," his father had said when he asked what it was. While diving for quarters at the bottom of the pool, Isaac had seen the bracelet circling Natalie's ankle.

Sometimes his father held his mother's hand when they walked along the greenbelt. His mother's hands were soft with faint blue veins. He saw their hands clasp, then unclasp, and worry knotted up in his chest.

The dry cleaner's window was drifted with fake snow. White Christmas lights chased each other around the marquee. Steam rose off the roof.

The last time Isaac had seen Mr. Branch was under the little green tent after Natalie's funeral. He had a scooped-out look.

Isaac cradled the smoked ham up the steps. His cast would come off next week and his father said his arm would be good as new. Sometimes at night, though, it still throbbed. He saw the stick arm from the dream but tossed it away.

The sign on the glass door said closed, but Mr. Branch saw them and waved, then came around the counter and opened the door. He'd gotten fatter since the funeral. His eyes were slits. He patted Isaac's shoulder as he stepped inside. The air was warm and moist. There was Christmas music playing somewhere.

Mr. Branch took the ham from Isaac and thanked them both. Too kind, he said. He asked Isaac what Santa was bringing him, but his slit-eyes wandered off Isaac and out into the dark parking lot. Then Isaac's father asked how he was doing and Mr. Branch said really pretty well, except, of course, for losing his daughter forever and ever. But you couldn't have everything, Mr.

Branch said. They stood there, not talking. In the back, cleaning machines hissed. Through a gap in a curtained doorway, Isaac could see a row of shiny black sewing machines. Then Mr. Branch apologized and said it was the wrong thing to say. That he'd been saying the wrong thing a lot lately. Mr. Branch pulled a plastic bag of clothes off the rack and pressed a button that sent the other clothes humming around.

"It's a hard time," Isaac's father said.

"There was that trouble years ago," Mr. Branch said, as if answering a question. "You remember that." He looked at Isaac's father. "When we went camping," he said. He looked at Isaac. "Natalie loved to camp." Then Mr. Branch seemed to catch himself. Isaac's father said he'd brought the paperwork they'd talked about and Mr. Branch said he was a true friend. He took a big swig of something from a cup on the counter and then walked over and emptied the register into a little metal box. He grabbed the ham and motioned Isaac and his father to the back of the shop and then down some stairs. Pipes stuck from the walls and ran in every direction. Near the bottom of the stairs, Mr. Branch looked back over his shoulder at them and stumbled and fell. He hit his knee hard against a step. The ham thumped to the bottom. Mr. Branch cursed and said for Isaac to pardon his French. Isaac's father helped Mr. Branch into the office. Mr. Branch grunted and made puffing sounds. It was warmer than upstairs and smelled slightly sweet. Isaac could hear the overhead pipes gurgling. There was a cot in the corner of the room and a metal shelf full of books. Photos of Natalie hung on the wall above it. One had scallop shells glued along the frame. In the photo, a younger Natalie posed in the pool with a bathing cap on, pretending to be in a water ballet. She had one arm thrown over her head in a ta-da motion. The half-smile on her face made her look like she knew something you didn't. A smart-aleck smile, his father would say. Isaac wondered if she'd meant it. In Isaac's school photos, his face was always different from what he meant.

From upstairs, the Christmas music made a tiny sound, as if they were underwater. Mr. Branch sat on the bed with pants rolled up, rubbing his knee. He'd tossed the money box on the bed and the change had slipped out.

Mr. Branch took the packet of legal papers from Isaac's father. They talked about other papers he'd need, but Isaac's father said they didn't need to get into them now. What they needed, he said, was some ice on that knee. Mr. Branch smiled and patted his father's thigh. "You loved her, too, didn't you?"

Isaac's father looked at Mr. Branch. "We all did," he said.

Mr. Branch eased back on the cot and lay among the papers and the spilled money and closed his eyes.

The pipes hissed and gurgled. Isaac looked at his father, who was looking up at the photos of Natalie. What was he thinking? At a Fourth of July picnic once, Isaac remembered seeing his father through the kitchen window talking with Natalie. His face was far away.

Someone yelled hello down the basement stairs: the deliveryman. Isaac's father looked over at Mr. Branch, who had his mouth open, and told Isaac they would need to help Mr. Branch lock up.

While his father locked the upstairs doors, Isaac came back downstairs to give Mr. Branch a baggie of ice for his knee. The office was dark. When Isaac turned on the light, Mr. Branch was sprawled on his stomach, naked on the cot. He looked to Isaac like an animal without its shell. Mr. Branch sat up and struggled to his feet. He grabbed his pants from the floor. Isaac could see shiny round tattoos on his thighs and belly. Then, several at a time, the tattoos fell away and plinked and rolled along the floor and Isaac realized they were coins.

* * *

On the way home, they turned down 37th Street. Thick strands of Christmas lights stretched over the road between houses. His father turned off the headlights and they crept slowly along the street because that's what you did here. It was like magic. The audience helped the magician and the magician helped the audience. It said this in all the magic books. *Would you please dim the lights? Would you please remain silent during the performance? Presto*. And people disappeared. Or they were cut into pieces. But then *Ta-da* they came back again the way they were. His father said Mr. Branch would pull himself together. But it took time to get over something like this. He was sorry Isaac had to see Mr. Branch in that condition.

Mr. Branch's pale naked body rose off the cot again and again the coins plinked and rolled.

The sidewalks and street were crowded. Peoples' faces were lit up by the glow. Every so often, some staring-up somebody would wander up against the side of his father's car and Issac would feel a sudden, soft bump.

18

So many handsome men, says Amaranta, a seamstress from the dry cleaners. Natalie wonders how Amaranta knew to look for her here. If it wasn't for the Chevy Blazer, she thinks, she'd be home now. Instead, she's down in some creek bed, the vintage dress she wore to the movie muddied, torn at the sleeve. A shoe lost in the scrub cedar. Anger tightens her throat.

Amaranta says Natalie must have been the first one on the dance floor and the last one off. It is certainly hard to choose, Amaranta says, her voice a mix of envy and disapproval. Natalie tries to explain there wasn't a dance, only a movie. Amaranta fingers the torn sleeve and scolds Natalie for her carelessness. Amaranta agrees—just this one time—to reweave the frayed threads. Natalie hears Amaranta's sewing machine whir to life, the teasing voices of Amaranta's two sisters who join in to help, their hands singing like crickets along the seams.

El guapo, the first sister says.

The second one nods her head. That's what I'm telling you. *Goddamn*, girl. You need a good-looking one. Like in the movies.

Yes, the first sister says, but if he's too good-looking you will have to put up with his horseshit.

Natalie had gone with a boy from class that night to see a new print of *The Third Man* at the Paramount Theater. Orson Welles as the mysterious Harry Lime.

Amaranta looks up from the dress. Oh, right. Orson

Welles. He was very fat.

He was handsome once, Natalie says.

We were all something once, Amaranta says.

The second sister says, I had a boyfriend one time who was so fat I'd always have to be on top. I would have dreams sometimes that he would roll over on me in my sleep and smother me like a little baby.

There's this scene in the movie, Natalie tells them, when you find out Orson Welles's character, Harry, is a murderer. Harry's old friend from school feels betrayed.

Old chum, the first sister says. That's what he would have said back then. Hey there, old chum.

Natalie keeps going: Is this the Harry he knew? The old friend wonders about this. But Harry's girlfriend, Anna, tells the old friend that people don't change just because you find out more. Anna doesn't just love Harry despite what he's done. She loves him regardless. Harry was real, she says. He wasn't just your friend and my lover, he was Harry.

The second sister nods. Love is fucked up that way, she says.

Who knows what made Mr. Orson Welles murder somebody? Amaranta says. You can't answer me that. But maybe, whatever it is, it's the same thing that made him love the girlfriend.

Or maybe, the first sister says, the murderer doesn't have anything to do with the old friend or the lover. He's filled up with all three, but he's empty at the same time, like an actor.

How do you know which is real? Natalie asks.

Amaranta says, I heard when Mr. Orson Welles passed away, his housekeeper showed up at this West Hollywood dry cleaners with the suit he wanted to be buried in. Mr. Orson Welles loved especially this beautiful blue brocade vest he once received from a lady admirer. Mr. Welles had not worn the vest in some time, the housekeeper said, but had wanted to again. The suit coat and vest would need significant alterations.

Amaranta smiles, then hunches back over her sewing machine. The whirring starts up again. So the housekeeper, Amaranta says, handed the tailor Mr. Orson Welles's measurements. The poor tailor tried to hide his surprise but dropped a pair of embroidery scissors to the floor. The housekeeper said it was true Mr. Welles was a man of enormous appetites. These appetites, whatever the joys and terrors they brought in life, tended in the end to separate such people from others. The housekeeper asked the tailor to use discretion in his work. So, after the housekeeper left, the tailor cut the material, did his work, just as I am now, Amaranta says.

Natalie hears the front door of the dry cleaner's chime open. She thinks, *Someone is here.*

When the tailor had finished the alterations, Amaranta says, and hung the brocade vest on the rack, he discovered it was the largest garment they had ever seen. The tailor made a $100 bet that three men could fit inside the vest. Another tailor said, not a chance. They gave it a try. They brought in the two delivery men and the cashier. It turned out there was room for one more. So the first tailor hopped in. They fastened the buttons. Mr. Orson Welles's blue brocade vest held all four of them inside.

Is there some kind of moral to this story? the second sister asks.

We are trying to help Natalie, Amaranta scolds.

Again, the front door chimes. Natalie can hear a tinny country song playing somewhere. Is someone here? Natalie asks.

Amaranta is finished with Natalie's dress. She brushes it off with a little black broom and lifts it onto the rack.

The light is falling in the room. It's the magic hour, Natalie thinks, the watery last minutes of the day movie people love because there are no shadows. On film, everything—landscapes, faces, objects—seems lit up from inside.

The dress hangs above Natalie. It isn't her vintage one at all but someone's wedding dress, a pearly brocade at the throat.

19

After Natalie left us, we laid awake nights listening to the scorpions' dry-leaf rustling in our light fixtures and vents. Driven into our houses by the flooding, they'd find their way down and curl in shoes by the door and dream of our feet. Their stings made our tongues and lips tingle afterward, taste like pennies, as if we were under some spell. When we crushed them with our heels, their bodies made twig-snapping sounds. We winced with pleasure at having something heroic to do.

Mornings, we nudged leaden sons and daughters out of beds and tried to revive our flat-lined hearts. Our children off to school, we drank coffee and stared out at storm-stripped trees, thinking we heard music again from Odie's open window. Snatches of old standards we'd always hated because they were our parents' songs but which we now missed. It's only a paper moon, sailing over a cardboard sea, *we hummed in our heads, but couldn't remember the rest.*

Late afternoon, our children returned, their needy, incessant mouths ticktocking us along. This boy, that girl, hurt feelings, it all ran together. We grew tired.

Gone, Odie had begun to seem more with us than before. His hands, greedy and benevolent. When a dog or cat turned up missing, our children said Odie was lonely and needed a friend. When small bills and change disappeared off nightstands, Odie was to blame. Then some children playing along the creek discovered the shoe tree: a rough cedar post set into the bank and nail-hung with partnerless shoes—a red pump, workboot, tennis shoe, yellow golash. The shoe tree looked, from across the creek, like a kind of ragged maypole, and from farther back still, say from Ruth Dodd's upstairs bedroom window, like the motley figure of a man, waving. We laughed it off, thinking our older sons had nailed it together as a prank. Still, we wondered about Odie.

*Our children, some brokenhearted, began to leave notes for Odie inside the shoes. Remembering Natalie's mother passing out fliers at the pool—*have you seen this young woman?—*a few children asked Odie why he took Natalie with him*. Was she teaching him to swim? *Whenever a pet was lost or a silver quincenera locket with a favorite aunt's picture disappeared, they'd scribble out notes to Odie pleading for its return. When Mark Soto's iguana went missing from its terrarium and no one found it in the usual places, Mark put a note inside a green converse high-top. Two days later, a next-door neighbor spotted the iguana high up in the Soto's backyard pecan tree where a storm-broken branch had fallen onto a power line. Blue sparks leaped onto the Sotos' roof. Mark Soto said Odie had sent the iguana back to save them. His mother, less generous, said she wished Odie would come clean up the mess.*

Some of the older children said there was a right way and a wrong way to write the notes, sounding like Jesuits. Many scribbled notes in secret, asking lost loves to call, or divorced parents to be reunited. Others asked for things they hadn't lost at all but still somehow missed. And even a few of us, on evening walks, might veer off the path and down to the tree, saying we just wanted to see what all the fuss was about.

After awhile, we wanted the shoe tree gone. It was an eyesore, we said. We talked of injuries, tetanus from the rusty nails. Liability. But behind our sweep-the-driveway-clear thoughts, we suspected the tree promised what we couldn't: the past restored, bitter feelings resolved, regrets made fewer. The story Odie told was curling back onto itself like a dry leaf. We clung to it because we lacked the courage to tell our own. Sometimes we hid from these thoughts in solitude and forgetfulness, sometimes in lovers' arms. We were afraid. There seemed no end to our responsibility.

***

If you jogged along our street some early morning in December, as Dennis Lipsy was now, you'd flatten red oak leaves that smelled of smoke, stride through low-slung pockets of cold air near the creek that might remind you of those long-ago winter mornings, the last doleful moments before the school bus arrived. Nine months from now, when Isaac dreams of people jumping from tall buildings before they do, Dennis will no doubt think back to Issac's own falling and broken arm. Dennis's absence. Years later, Dennis might confuse the telling of it, even to himself, cut out parts that don't fit. But we know this cutting is part of the story, too, and what is missing makes up much of our own story.

Along Lake Austin Boulevard, we see Dennis jogging in place at the curb, keeping his heart rate up, waiting for cars to pass. He checks his watch. In a moment, he'll scissor-leg down the path to the pool, where he'll glance over, out of habit, to Natalie's lifeguard chair. He'll catch himself as he does it, then look steadily ahead. He'll forget this gesture by the end of his run, just as we would.

What if all our involuntary gestures were photographed

and then laid side by side? Would they tell our alternative histories? Reveal thoughts that did not quite become acts but instead worked away secret and silent inside us?

As if Dennis hears us on the trail, there's an awkward catch in his stride, like gravel has slipped inside his shoe.

IV

20

Dennis was sixteen. He and Billy Mueller were headed to a party. They'd stopped off to pick up Sonny Farbrother's daughter, Margo. When she climbed into the car, she looked hard at Dennis in the backseat as if trying to place him. Dennis waved awkwardly, said hi, disheartened she hadn't remembered him but a little relieved, too. Margo turned to Billy Mueller, who was driving, and gave him a sour look, like the night had suddenly turned on her. Billy's shoulders were too small for the rest of him. They belonged on a child. His shoulders had been that way—behind the rest of him—since Dennis could remember. Billy got laid more than anyone, though, it seemed to Dennis, even with his affliction. He knew things.

No one could remember the name of the person who was having the party. Dennis guessed if you knew whose house it was, maybe you'd feel worse about messing it up. He stared off at Sonny's little stone house, where a string of green Christmas lights blinked around the big front window. He could see Sonny inside at the table, cracking open pecan shells, watching TV. Dennis hadn't seen Sonny since Sonny had slammed a college boy's head with the car door the year before. After that, Dennis's parents had forced him to quit the import shop. Dennis had written Sonny telling him he probably had good reasons for what he did. But all he'd gotten back from him was a $125 check for the painting he'd done.

Like her dad, Margo was long-legged and her skin was as

dark and smooth as polished pecan. She had taken a bus down from Oklahoma just as she had the previous Christmas when Dennis had first seen her working the register at the import shop, only this time, apparently, she was staying. Margo had even caught him staring at her a few times through the shop window while he scraped paint from the side of the building. He remembered thinking she looked older than him, though he found out later she was the same age, fifteen. Around Sonny, Margo was serious and there was very little small talk. They were wary of one another, it seemed, after spending so much time apart, though Sonny claimed they had a special bond. "I buried the stem of her umbilical cord under a persimmon tree like the old people said to, you know. And, so when I came to Texas, I had the tree dug up and planted out back to keep her and me close. It doesn't much like the soil here, though." Margo, as if to spite Sonny, flirted openly with the men who came in the shop. She would squeeze a man's arm, hover near his shoulder, toss back her hair and laugh with her high cheekbones at something that struck her as funny and that she would share only with him. She and Dennis had talked around the checkout counter and she'd gotten Dennis's last name wrong, calling him Louis, and it stuck for some reason. "Hey there, Smokin' Joe Louis," she'd say when he came up to the register to help customers to their cars with chimeneas or ornamental bird baths.

And when Dennis had stayed late one night to help unload a Mexican pottery truck, Margo had pressed against him in the truck's narrow canvas-covered bed, her arms encircling his waist. Dennis held a goat-shaped pot in one hand. He stood perfectly still. She smelled like the waffle cakes at the River Festival. She kissed him on the mouth. And when she squeezed past him to grab a box of smiling crescent moons, her hand had brushed his crotch. She'd then headed out the back of the truck, down the ramp, into the glare of the floodlights.

Billy headed back up Sonny's dirt road, then pulled the car onto the highway. The Ramones' "I Wanna Be Sedated" thumped out of speakers near Dennis's head. Billy leaned over and said something close to Margo's ear that made her glance back quickly and laugh. Dennis's face burned. He looked out the window at the exposed layers of limestone where the road cut through. He tried to think of something clever to say that would humiliate Billy but all his thoughts dried up.

Billy pulled out a Coke bottle with Wild Turkey in it from under the seat and handed it to Margo. She took a drink, then passed it back to Dennis. "Hey, I remember you," Margo said suddenly, her face brightening. "Smokin' Joe Louis."

"How's Sonny?" Dennis said.

"Not well. Sonny's a sick man." She took the bottle back and took another drink. "He wanted me to stay home tonight, but I just said, got some plans, Geronimo."

"That's good," Dennis said, and then wondered why he said it.

Billy said, "You bet it's good." He reached across and did something with his hand Dennis couldn't see and Margo laughed and told him to stop.

Dennis drank from the bottle and looked out the window at the hills, their purple ridges, wishing he could get out and walk home.

***

The college boy had called Margo a cunt. That's not where it started, only where Dennis came in. He'd been on a ladder caulking the sides of the import shop, when the boy drove up in his maroon Firebird and went inside. *Cunt*. It sounded sharp and final. Then something banged against the inside wall where Dennis was caulking. It made the ladder shake. He could hear the radio inside playing Sam and Dave's "Soothe Me." More yelling. Then the back door had banged open and Sonny had followed the college boy out to his car, quick long strides crunching over gravel. What happened next was unclear. Dennis couldn't remember which things he'd actually seen or which things he'd heard about later.

Thunk. That was the sound he heard as he came around the corner of the shop, caulking gun in hand. The sound of metal on bone.

The college boy was sitting on the gravel next to his Firebird, holding his head, blubbering softly. Long blonde hair hung in his face. Blood spattered the front of his shirt. Margo circled the car, her gaze shifting between Sonny and the boy. Sonny was quiet, standing beside the open driver's side door, running his hands through his gray-streaked hair. "Well, Goddamn," Sonny said matter-of-factly, tossing up his hands like someone whose horse had lost. He sighed, looked at Dennis holding the caulking gun. "Don't shoot," he said, then looked out at a knot of cedars and some rusted machine parts sticking out of the bunch grass. The college boy whimpered. Margo crouched near the front of the Firebird, came toward the boy on all fours. "Go away now, Daddy," she said in a low pleading voice. Sonny walked over and kicked the boy in the side. He yelped. Sonny wouldn't let Margo go near him. He slung handfuls of gravel at her until she went back in the shop. Then Sonny had turned to Dennis and said, "We look like crazy people, don't we?" and, not waiting for an answer, had gone inside. Dennis had waded through the bunch grass and cactus, and walked home before the EMS and police came. He didn't tell anyone he was there, offered no witness. Sonny was in the Travis County Jail for four months for assault.

Later, Dennis would hear of Sonny telling friends how he'd listened to his cellmate, a man convicted of killing his own child, bawling like a baby for nights on end before they'd taken him off to the state prison in Huntsville. The man pleaded with Sonny to believe that he hadn't killed the toddler, that the boy had fallen from a retaining wall onto his head. "He was sleepy afterwards," the man had told him, "so I let him sleep." Though Sonny followed the case and knew the preponderance of evidence stacked against the man, a fiction was all the man asked of him. Sonny said it was a small gift to give.

When Sonny retells parts of this story to Dennis on his visits now, twenty-two years later, he leaves out sections and adds others. Dennis corrects him. Sonny says, "Well, who the hell doesn't elaborate to get their point across? The Sermon on the Mount? The Raising of Lazarus? Shit. Come on now. You can't kid a kidder."

* * *

At the party, Dennis and Margo sat around a backyard bonfire passing a joint she had pulled from her change purse. It was late and cold and they'd lost track of Billy an hour ago, not long after he sampled some pills from a bathroom medicine cabinet. Other faces were nearby: Sean Weakes, robed in a blanket, his arm around Lucinda Bisson, two people Dennis had known off and on since elementary school but hadn't spoken to in years. He nodded to them, said hello.

A group was on the roof of the house shooting off bottle rockets. Each time one exploded overhead, a dog howled mournfully from its pen at the edge of the yard. The dog's eyes shone yellow in the firelight.

"We should look for Billy," Margo said.

"You worried about him?" Dennis asked.

"Billy's special," Margo said. "He's our ride."

Dennis was quiet for a little while, then he said, "Are y'all together?"

"Billy and me? Naw, he just makes me laugh."

"Billy says y'all are."

"He says that, huh?" Margo took a hit off the joint, coughed.

"He says that you're going to Las Vegas together and work in the casinos."

"You believe that?" Margo asked.

"No. I don't know. Billy says things," Dennis said.

"You boys," Margo said and laughed.

Dennis laughed too, but his heart wasn't in it. She had a way of saying it that made you feel small.

Margo's eyes followed the cinders rising from the fire. She was quiet for a while. Tree sap popped and sizzled. Dennis could hear a Rolling Stones' song playing inside the house. Then Margo said, "When I was seven, I had these migraines. None of the doctors could explain it. They did spinal taps, thinking it might be meningitis." She licked her fingers and pinched the joint out. "Sonny was never around. And my mom had to go to work, so on bad days my older cousin Cecilia would stay with me and put cold washcloths on my head, feed me aspirin. She'd sing me songs, too. Church songs." Margo sang softly:

When my feeble life is over
time for me will be no more
Guide me gently, safely over,
to that farther shore

"Except I thought it was *father* shore." She smiled.

"Was this on the reservation?" Dennis asked.

"What?"

"Sonny said you lived on a reservation."

"He's so full of shit." Margo said.

"He said you and your mother still lived there."

"We never did. We live in an apartment building in Tulsa."

Dennis stoked the fire with a stick. He hated Sonny, he decided.

"Anyway, when I'd have these migraines, I'd get delirious from the pain. Have nightmares but be awake. Sometimes, I'd look out the window and see Sonny waving up at me from the street. He'd have a blue sport coat on and be young and good-looking like when he was in the movies and he'd say, 'come on down and give me a kiss', because he's such a liar." Margo paused. In the flickering light her face seemed ashen. Dennis wanted to touch her hair.

"And once, when my mom was off visiting my grandma in Lawton, I had this real bad one. Poor old Cecilia tried the washcloths and songs but nothing worked. The neighbors heard all this crying and screaming and not knowing the story, they started banging on ceilings and floors with whatever was handy. And then some shit-for-brains yelled up through the vents he'd come up there and shut me up. A door slammed. This scared poor old Cecilia so much she grabbed my hand and out we went into the hall and through a door I'd never even seen, up some dark, pee-smelling stairs. I looked down and saw Sonny at the bottom, hands cupped to his mouth like he was calling up at me. But instead of words, feathers were coming out." Margo paused. The wind picked up and ash from the fire dusted her lap and Margo brushed it off. "So me and Cecilia ran faster. Then I heard somebody bawling. Cecilia told me to shut up and yanked my arm. Then we went through another door. We stepped into blue sky. Pigeons exploded around us. A huge white woman's face smiled down at me. Gleaming teeth. Then I saw the cars and people way down below. We'd left them behind. Cecilia had taken me to Heaven. 'Are other kids here?' I asked her. Cecilia just stared at me. 'Will you hush?' she said. I noticed her shaking. I remember wondering if we'd have different names in heaven. We sat there on the roof until the sky went dark and the lights came on below and we didn't say anything. Just waited to see what would happen. After a while, I noticed my migraine was just a dull ache and that I had to pee. Then me and Cecilia got up and made our way across the rooftops and down through another door and stairwell and found Cecilia's stepmother in her apartment, cooking Tuna Helper. We'd gone and come back, I remember thinking. But nothing had changed. Things went back to the way they were before. I wasn't different."

Margo looked hard at Dennis. "You think things are set up a certain way, Joe Louis, but they aren't. You can't change what's coming by being one place or the other. So you might as well pretend you chose it that way."

"Lie, you mean," Dennis said.

She smiled. "Was my story true or not?"

"I don't know," he said. "It sounded true."

"Then it doesn't make any difference, one way or the other, does it?"

Margo leaned forward and kissed him. Molasses and ash filled his mouth. She pressed into him. He ran his hand up under her jacket, touched the warm skin of her belly. An erection swelled awkwardly in his jeans. "Goddamn, your hands are cold," she said after a minute, pulling her jacket down.

A boy in his underwear came across the lawn carrying an

end table and couch cushions. It wasn't until he stood in front of the fire that Dennis recognized him as Billy Mueller.

"Billy?" Margo said.

"Yeah?" Billy wheeled around, dragging the cushion along the ground.

"What the hell are you doing?" Margo said. "Where are your clothes for Christ sakes?"

"Just keeping y'all warm," he said, matter-of-factly, and tossed his armload in the fire. A cheer went up from the roof. Flames licked at the end table's varnish for a few seconds and then rose. "Hey, Lucinda," Billy said and stood there canting his bony hips, as if he would say more but then didn't. Billy's face was ecstatic. Lucinda Bisson laughed. Billy raised a fist in salute, then headed back across the lawn.

"We should get him in the car," Margo said, rising, following Billy.

"Sure," Dennis said, but he sat there for awhile, his head sodden with Margo. Sonny stood in a dark stairwell somewhere, his mouth full of feathers.

Across from him, Sean and Lucinda's faces were hidden by the blanket, a pair of monks. Bits of ash from the couch cushion fell softly on them, like snow.

He stood up and headed toward the house. Another rocket exploded and the dog started up again. On the porch, Mark Sievers, a sallow-faced boy from Dennis's English class, asked him how it was going. Sievers's eyes were jittery. He rubbed his sideburns and mouth with his fingers. Dennis said it was going all right and started to squeeze by him to the sliding glass door. "You getting any out there?" Sievers asked. Through the glass door, Dennis could see the deserted living room. Bottles and trash everywhere. A knot of people now stood in the entryway. He could see Margo there, looking down at something. Sievers said, "You know about her, right?" Dennis looked at him. "Her and her daddy," Sievers said, making a circle with his index finger and poking his other index finger through it. Dennis's stomach grabbed. "You're a goddamn liar," Dennis said, though he knew it was true and that he'd known it for some time. He shouldered Sievers out of the way and headed into the house, which was thick with smoke and the smell of spilled beer. Someone had smashed the dining room light fixture. The bare metal rod hung at an odd angle from the ceiling. Broken eggshells of glass lay on the linoleum. In the entryway, where the crowd gathered, Billy, still in his underwear, was bent over a fat boy, giving him mouth to mouth. Billy looked up, a string of saliva swinging from his bottom lip. His eyes were shiny from whatever he'd taken. For a second, he glanced around and seemed to forget his task, seized by the shine of that other world. Then he started on the boy again. Dennis watched the rise and fall of Billy's child shoulders. No one seemed to know who the fat boy was. He drove a red Ford pickup, someone said. He'd come late, made a pass at Taeger Sutfin's girlfriend, and then he and Sutfin had gotten into it. Before anybody threw a punch, though, the fat boy collapsed there in the entryway with a thud.

Margo was down beside Billy, tugging at her hair. Dennis closed his eyes. Opened them. His heart thudded crazily. His face felt tight and swollen from the heat of the bonfire as if he were outgrowing his own skin.

Billy's lips were sealed around the fat boy's. They shared the same air. At any moment it seemed the boy's jowly cheeks might suck Billy in. Billy breathed deeply into him once, twice, and then the fat boy opened his eyes. "Rise," Billy said. "Rise and walk."

21

The changes in P.G. after the accident confused him at first. His tooth stopped hurting, though he'd put off the root canal. He'd lost seven pounds, yet he'd never had a bigger appetite. The dreams he used to have, at least the ones he could remember, had always seemed like B-movies in which all the characters made him feel small. But lately he'd had dreams about the girl, Natalie, that left him with an odd elated feeling when he woke. She would often appear to him dressed in other people's clothes. Sometimes his mother's, sometimes old friends'. Lately she'd come to him in the green camisole and jeans of a former girlfriend from college. He hadn't thought about the girlfriend in some time—her hard gymnist thighs and east Texas drawl. Her lack of inhibitions had scared him at first. "Mr. McWhirter, why don't we have a little bit too much to drink?" she'd say and later that night he'd find himself nearly in a fight with some regular at the Deep Eddy Cabaret over an insult she'd hurled. Afterwards, when they'd walk back towards her parents' house, adrenaline buzzing in their heads, she'd insist on making love on the darkened municipal golf course. Or other times, on the way home from a movie or concert, they'd abruptly pull off the highway into a rest stop and do it in his car with the seats flattened back, and she would make a production of gripping the lip of the open sunroof, raising her naked body gracefully over his, her legs V'd spectacularly, and then slowly lowering herself onto him. Her athlete's face turned to him, concentrated, serene.

Passing car headlights flared off her shoulders and breasts and he'd feel as if he were somehow singled out for this vision.

He supposed one reason he hadn't thought of the girlfriend in so long was that, near the end of things, he'd humiliated her at a party. He'd drunkenly accused her of making a pass at his best friend, although he knew the friend had initiated it. P.G. and the girlfriend had argued in the front yard. Then he'd gotten in his car and driven slowly away. She'd followed, run yard to yard, begging him to come back. She hadn't done anything, she'd yelled. As he was about to turn around in someone's driveway, satified, he supposed, with whatever suffering he'd caused her, she tripped over a sprinkler head and knocked out a tooth.

In the dreams, Natalie would confide in him that she had loved and lost, too. Sometimes she would pull out her tooth for a joke. Other times she came to P.G. dressed in his mother's old spattered painting smock, smelling of pity and forgiveness, and they'd paint together on his parents' sun porch just as he had when he was seven. Natalie would narrow her eyes at the canvas. "A little more blue," she'd tell him and he'd dab his brush in the paint and then touch it lightly—a caress, she'd say—to a figure in a brocade vest.

22

Every Jesus needs a Judas, Jones says.

Odie shuffles a deck of cards and fans them on the table.

I just thought my Judas would be, well, a little more together, I guess, Jones says. No offense.

Choose a card, Odie says.

Jones slides a card from the deck. But here we are, he says. An old familiar pair of shoes. Jones looks down at Odie's bare feet.

Now, Odie says, commit your card to memory. Then place it back in the deck.

Do you miss her? Jones asks.

Ruth? Yes, terribly, Odie says. But I can't get back for some reason.

Jones looks at his card, then puts it back. She's keeping a vigil, you know, he says. Raveling and unraveling your clothes. And here you are doing card tricks.

Sleight of hand, Odie says, correcting him. Odie reshuffles.

In old Persia, Odie, they knew something about love. In fact, they considered Satan God's greatest lover. But as an angel Satan wouldn't bow down to man. Satan said, goddamn, God, what would I do that for when I love you so much? It seemed coarse, bowing to this little old nothing, man. I mean, God was Satan's thing. God was what ran in his veins. So when Satan wouldn't bow, God said, okay, that's it. Begone, motherfucker.

And he threw him out of heaven. But down there in hell, with all that fire and bad coffee, you know what kept him going? The memory of God's lovely awful voice saying get out of my sight. Satan held onto it. Would suffer any pains. Now, friend, that's love.

But who can live off a memory?

Jones lights a cigar. Plenty of people, he says. For instance, you.

Odie drums the cards with his fingers. Mothers putting cups of the stuff to their lips, Odie says. All the little ones, dead. That stuck with me.

It wasn't easy, believe me. They cried up a storm.

And then they didn't.

I did it out of love, Odie. Let this cup pass from me, He said, but it wouldn't.

Selfless, Odie says. Always looking out for the other fellow.

Jones draws on his cigar. And what about you? Running off because you can't get the ending right?

The thing had already happened, Odie says.

Sure. But what about us? Afterward? Two people minding their own business. That dead sea of devotion before us. Our eyes met.

I lifted the gun.

Those cicadas were some kinda loud. Surprised it didn't put your concentration off.

I pulled the trigger.

A kiss. Fireworks.

Odie studies the cards, then looks up at Jones. Is the Queen of spades your card? Odie asks.

Well look at that. Son of a bitch. You found it.

23

Every time he jogged past the creek, Dennis half-expected to see Odie's pale arm waving in the current, a parody of the hundreds of evening waves Odie had given from the street while walking arm-in-arm with Ruth. Hadn't he and Winnie imitated Odie and Ruth's evening walks? Tried to conjure older, more contented selves? Hadn't they expected to grow old together? Faults smoothed over or sympathized with, understandings reached? Their shared teasing about his graying hair and growing near-sightedness, her long stretches of reticence and longing for another child—weren't these gentle preludes to some greater intimacy? But it struck him now he and Winnie had hidden from themselves the most obvious consequence of their growing old together: in the end, one of them would be abandoned as Ruth Dodd was now.

***

The letter from Winnie's daughter Allison had come on Wednesday. Dennis had stared at it on the table, already opened, a photo sticking from it.

Winnie had been planning Allison's visit to Austin after Christmas, restaurants she and Dennis might take her to, sightseeing they would do. Winnie had even bought Allison a maternity dress and mailed it to her in Alaska. But Dennis worried about the changes the visit might bring on. Winnie's expectations.

Inside the letter were photos of Allison in wading boots on the deck of a boat, holding a fish as long as her arm. Her red hair whipped sideways. Her face angular and handsome, almost boyish, nothing like Winnie's. The eyes, though, he imagined, were hazel like Winnie's, with flecks of brown. Allison seemed to be glancing at something just outside the photo frame. Dennis remembered the biologist's stricken face and wondered if it lay beneath the face Allison wore in the photo.

Dennis told Winnie to be careful, go slow.

Winnie said nineteen years was slow enough.

After they told Isaac about Allison, he'd asked to send her a photo of himself in his baseball uniform. That way, Isaac said, she would know what she was getting into.

And what had Dennis gotten into? Sometimes, late at night, he'd be working in their den on a living will or bankruptcy filing and the close lotion and chlorine smell of Natalie's bedroom closet would fill his nostrils. He'd feel again the welcome weight of her clothes, pinning him in. Then the watery pressure would build in his ears. His heart would race and he'd have to go outside on the porch to catch his breath.

24

The sun-spattered room listed to one side, then Allison righted it.

The midwife, a squat, large-breasted woman who insisted they sit on pillows along the floor, asked Allison about her family history. Allison explained that she was adopted, she'd never known her real parents. Certain hereditary traits could cause problems, the midwife said. Rh blood factor, for instance. The mother's antibodies attack the child's blood cells.

The midwife repositioned herself on her pillow, patted Allison's knee. "Probably nothing to worry about," she said. "It's just sometimes the body has plans of its own."

The room heaved as if they'd hit a trough. Allison's cigarettes and lip balm spilled from her purse. She nodded for some reason, quickly stuffed them back in, told the midwife most of the time her body was planning to throw up. On the wall behind the midwife, photos of Inuit children the midwife had delivered in remote villages outside of Juneau. One of the children had the sloped forehead of Down's. "Those are all my little ones," the midwife said. Allison could feel the midwife watching her. Allison asked about the details of home birth, possible complications. The midwife told her she always took reasonable precautions—for instance, notifying the hospital in advance in case anything went wrong. But what were reasonable precautions? Allison wondered. Could you stave off calamity? She didn't know. She and the midwife sat in silence for a few moments.

"Do you have a partner?" the midwife asked and for a moment Allison drew a blank. Partner? She thought of people dancing. Partners in crime. "Oh. You mean Zach."

"Will he be coming to birthing class with you?"

She heard the nervous hum in Zach's throat just before he spoke. "Maybe," she said.

The midwife looked up from the paper she was filling out, fiddled with an earring. "Are things a little iffy between you two?"

Iffy. Jiffy. Midwifey. She was sweating. Nausea roiled through her.

"It happens. The fathers sometime freak out. How long have you been together?"

Allison focused on the midwife's earring, a spiraling crystal, no, a snake. "Awhile," Allison said, absently. She breathed in and out slowly, trying to will her stomach calm. Tasted saltine crackers at the back of her throat. "Since we were young," Allison said, then realized how strange it must sound since she was only nineteen. She looked off at the Inuit children, the Down's child. An old grainy grade school science film flickered though her head, cartoon blood cells dressed as knights in armor, jousting.

25

In his dream, Isaac is back in his hospital bed. He can feel his arm shrinking until it is nothing but a bony stick to hang feathers on. He hears something tapping against the window wanting in or out. Which is it? He's not sure. Through the gap in the curtain, he can see sparrows. They rise and fall and rise again, as if each one tugs the other by an invisible string. He gets out of bed and goes to the window. Some of the sparrows catch the sun on the way down and are beautiful. Then he realizes they aren't sparrows at all but swirling sheets of paper. Homework and phone bills and e-mails and love letters and certificates. Everyday things that once belonged to people and want to again. They keep coming down. There's no end to them. Like the time he'd left the spigot running in his backyard and made a giant pool. He feels shame wash through him as he realizes he has needed to pee for a long time and now pee is warming his pajama leg and pooling warmly at his feet.

The paper swirls and finally floats down. It blankets the cars in the parking lot and drifts up the playscape slide. A blizzard. He tries to tell his mother. Waves his withered wing-arm. Well, that's really something, his mother says, not even looking up, only staring into her lap at the shiny pages of a fashion magazine.

V

26

Johan Hofzinser, Odie tells Jones, was the greatest sleight-of-hand magician of the nineteeth century. He was so astonishingly good some people said he was in league with the devil.

Ah, Jones says, nice. Building suspense. Is he or isn't he?

One night, Odie says, Hofzinser is having dinner in a Vienna restaurant with his fiancee and several members of Viennese society. But every time he starts to take a bite, one of the society ladies asks him to perform a card trick.

Sleight of hand, Jones says.

Right. So after refusing several requests, the magician finally agrees. He performs the Royal Confidant, Magic Trio. Old standbys. They clap politely but aren't amazed. He sets the cards aside, gives a sly look over to his fiance. She smiles back. There's love there, everyone thinks. One of the society members says what a wonderful smile she has. Enchanting. Do you think so? his fiancee says. Hofzinser passes a teacup to his fiancee and, one by one, she pulls out her teeth and plinks them down in the teacup. The society members are horrified. The fiancee passes the teacup down the table, so each can see, and then down to Hofzinser himself. He rattles them around in the cup, then places his napkin over it, mumbles something appropriately unintelligible, furrows his brow. A few seconds pass. His fiancee says for him to hurry up, she's getting hungry. A few more seconds pass. Ah, that's better, the fiancee says. And when the society members turn to look at her, she is smiling, her gleaming teeth restored.

It's only a trick, Jones says. There's no story. No plot. Worst of all, old Hofzinser doesn't even turn out to be the devil. No devilment.

But, Odie says, his sleight of hand floats like a brilliant balloon between them and the world. At night before bed and next day on the way to pick up the kids at piano lessons, the teacup full of teeth rises in their minds. How could we watch but not see? they wonder. Do our everyday lives—even the ways we miss them— escape us this way? Can these, too, be restored?

27

The counter girl at the vintage clothing shop had asked P.G. if he'd found what he was looking for. And because he'd drunk a half-dozen beers at happy hour with his middleman, Howard Brakhage, and because he'd looked unsuccessfully in five other vintage shops the week before, P.G. had almost told the counter girl about the dreams. Almost. But he'd kept himself in check. "Well," P.G. had said casually, "I do have my eye on something."

On the way home with the brocade vest, he'd driven past Charlotte Branch's house as he did nearly every evening now. He'd recently begun writing poems to Natalie in his head. Sometimes, though, the lines simply came to him, as if they'd been there all along. Waiting. Even while he worried over a particular vehicle's resale value or the hourly cycles of timed neighborhood street lights.

At home that night, Melinda had stroked the vest's silk, traced her finger over the embroidered geometric shapes, birds, flower vines. Arabesques, he'd explained to her. The Sufi mystics thought they got you closer to God.

Melinda stared at him.

He'd put the vest on, fastened the buttons. Stood in front of their bedroom mirror.

"You're really going to wear that?" Melinda said. She pulled at a loose thread along the shoulder of the vest. "It looks so old-timey," she said. "Like something a saloon piano player would wear."

"That's just what I'll do," he said, removing her hand from his shoulder. "I'll take up the piano." He winked at Melinda. Smiled.

In the mirror, under the recessed lights, P.G noticed that the vest had a deep blue sheen that reminded him of a scarab beetle's shell.

28

Sleet pecked the windows. Dennis lay naked beside Winnie in bed, pressure building in his ears. They had tried to make love but he'd lost his erection midway through. He couldn't focus. Winnie asked if it was something she'd done or not done but he explained it wasn't, he was just over-tired. Things at the office had gotten out of hand. Lionel Wallace hadn't shown for his court hearing and now Sonny Farbrother was making threatening phone calls to his daughter. Winnie said she was worried about Dennis. She said he should've gotten the flu shot like she'd asked him to. She rubbed her hand along his temple, kissed his shoulder. He turned toward her, kissed her hard on the mouth, ran his hands over her body, along her hips, and then, after awhile, slipped a hand down between her legs. She moved against him. When she finally came, he felt somehow on the other side of it, not there at all.

Asleep now, Winnie sighed heavily. She fluttered her hand above her face, as if an insect buzzed there. The heater clicked on and seemed louder than normal. Pipes gurgled in the walls. An old house getting older. He thought of Charlotte Branch, alone in her house. Saw her again in Natalie's bedroom after the funeral in September, putting Natalie's hat back on the bedpost, walking circles around the room. What was going through her mind now? Almost three months to the day since they found Natalie along the river and it still wasn't clear what had happened. Possible hit and run, they'd said. Neck and skull fractures. But how had she ended up in the river, caught like a kite in a tree?

At the Sotos' Christmas party a year ago, he remembered Natalie telling him a story about Groucho Marx going to a Hollywood séance. Madame Narobi, a kind of medium to the stars, claimed to speak to the greats of history, Natalie said. Sitting Bull, Alexander the Great, Cleopatra. Madame Narobi let the audience ask questions and she'd ferry the answer back from the great beyond. Reveal secrets they'd taken to the grave. Sometime midway through the séance Groucho's hand shot up. "Madame Narobi? What's the capital of North Dakota?"

At the party, he and Natalie had stood at the dessert table together. Natalie lifted up a piece of gingerbread. Passed her hand over it and pretended to say something in Latin. "Remember to remember me," she'd said, in a mock-solemn voice, and handed the gingerbread to him on a napkin.

"Why, where are you off to?" he'd joked. He'd glanced around the room. Winnie was standing near the big spruce tree in the living room, sipping wine, talking with Sally Rosenberg. Someone cackled from the kitchen.

Natalie said, "Maybe west. Maybe to film school. Haven't made up my mind."

Dennis's stomach fell. He looked at his drink glass, now empty. An image rose in his mind of Natalie in the Pattersons' kitchen that time, the disembodied hands running along her shoulders and arms.

"You've got a weird look on your face," Natalie said, pulling her hair from her eyes, staring at him with—Concern? Curiosity? He couldn't tell.

"Weird look?" His heart was thudding in his ears. He tried to calm himself.

"Yep," Natalie had said, biting into a piece of

gingerbread. "A look like you'd miss me."

In Dennis and Winnie's bedroom, the sleet pecked harder against the window. The wind came in gusts. The roads had already iced over.

Just before Christmas, he'd seen the SOLD sign in Charlotte Branch's yard. Then the boxes late this afternoon, stacked in the driveway, some even lined up out in the yard. In them somewhere, he imagined, Natalie's clothes, shoes, photos, movie posters, books. Charlotte not wanting the movers tracking in mud, he thought, her obsessive-compulsiveness grown stronger. Then, this afternoon, after he'd barely made it up the hill in the car himself, he'd seen the moving van stuck at the bottom, a back tire in the ditch. So now, the boxes squatted in rows on Charlotte's sloping lawn, gathering sleet like neglected monuments.

Beside Dennis in the bed, Winnie twitched in her sleep.

29

December evenings along the hike and bike trail, we'd sometimes see P.G. McWhirter wearing, beneath his suit coat, the blue brocade vest he wore in our living rooms, evangelizing about comprehensive life insurance policies. He'd splay open his black case on our coffee tables with actuarial certainty, his voice rising like a tremulous song. Those of us raised in the church thought of old paintings of John the Baptist clothed in animal skins, a fevered prophesy on his lips.

On the trail, P.G. would veer off near the expressway bridge and head down to Johnson Creek, where, our children said, he slipped squares of folded paper into the shoe tree. We imagined him mumbling something vaguely penitent and threatening. A few of the older children remembered lines from poems he'd written and placed there. My heart is a hollow muscular organ the size of your fist, *was one that looped in our heads.* He is in love, *we said. And began to see in his eyes, a look. A smoldering. Embers kicked from a fire. Others dismissed it, wrote down midlife crisis in the blank, remembering their own tentative passes at one another at holiday parties. A sad, furtive touching in hallways or guest rooms where jackets lay across the beds like shed skins.*

We wanted embers. We wanted to wrap ourselves in the bedroom curtains and set them ablaze.

30

"A scorpion stung me," Allison said, framed in Dennis and Winnie's bedroom doorway in a T-shirt and underwear. The hall light threw her rounded belly into relief. It was a little after 3:00 A.M. Her voice was shaky. "It got me on the hand but my lips feel funny," Allison said, touching them with her fingers. "Is that the last symptom before you drop dead?"

She'd arrived two days before, right after Christmas. She'd taken a bus from Seattle to Austin. Three days of sitting had made her calves and ankles swell. Elephantitus, she called it.

"The stings are harmless," Winnie said, rising out of bed. Dennis told her the tingling would go away after a little while.

"Well, they sure hurt like fuck," Allison said. She laughed nervously, touched her belly. "Someone's really kicking in there," she said. In the hall light, Winnie thought she could see the moving knot of a hand or foot under the T-shirt.

At the bus station two days before, Winnie had hugged her and Allison's tight belly had rubbed against Winnie's own. Allison had stiffened. Winnie imagined Allison thinking of a conch shell. Hard. Impervious. What had Winnie expected?

Dennis turned on the nightstand lamp.

"It won't affect the baby, right?" Allison said.

"Other than getting you upset, it won't," Winnie said, noticing Allison's breasts pushing at the T-shirt, the sheerness of her panties. "Sweetie, let's get you a robe and I'll put some ice on your hand."

Dennis asked where the scorpion had gone.

Allison said she hoped far the fuck away. "Jesus Christ," she said. "Ugh."

They gathered in the living room, while Dennis dumped the contents of Allison's suitcase on the floor. Sifted through her clothes and underwear. A fat scorpion sat curled beneath, on the wood floor. Dennis smashed it with a rolled magazine. Then they noticed, clinging to its broken back, a collection of little scorpions.

"That's a sight that might break someone's heart, but it won't be mine," Allison said.

The next night, New Year's Eve, they'd all gone out to dinner at an expensive Italian restaurant. Winnie and Allison talked about Allison's father, the marine biologist, who Winnie said she had seen by chance several years ago at the hospital. He was a pharmaceutical salesman now. There was more to tell, of course, but Winnie decided not to. There would be time. No reason to overwhelm her now. But Winnie also knew she wanted Allison to herself, that she was wishing the eddy of her past gone. While they were talking, Winnie had noticed one of Allison's eyes—hazel like her own—was set back a little farther than the other. Its coloring slightly off.

"Something wrong?" Allison said.

"Oh. Sorry. Just admiring you."

Across the table, Isaac was pestering Dennis for gelato.

"It's the eye," Allison said, matter-of-factly.

"You look really great," Winnie said. "Seven months and you're so tiny. Should have seen me." Her face grew hot.

"What about the eye?" Isaac asked across the table.

"It usually takes people a long time but your mom noticed right off," Allison said. "Doesn't quite have full range of motion either," Allison said. "See?" She moved her eyes side to side but the left one didn't follow.

Dennis told Isaac to leave his mom and Allison alone, asked what kind of gelato he wanted.

"Something only a mother would know, right?" Allison said. Her face was a blank.

Silence.

Then one of the waiters tripped and flung a tray of silverware to the floor. From then on, Winnie would associate it with the putting out of Allison's eye, though Allison would explain later that a toy airplane propeller had caused the damage when she was three.

"No big deal," Allison said. She smiled, cut her steak. "It's not hereditary."

Isaac said, "Is it glass?" and peered squint-eyed across the table at her.

"Nope. Plastic," Allison said. "From the wonderful people at Dupont." She tapped the cornea with her nail.

Forks still flinging in her head, Winnie changed the subject, talked about how they would take the paddleboat upriver that night to see the fireworks.

31

If you paid twenty dollars to drink champagne and take the paddleboat upriver on New Year's Eve, you might have seen, after the city fireworks ended, the fiery tails of bottle rockets arcing over our neighborhood. You'd point them out, as Dennis was now, gripped with nostalgia for long-ago New Year's Eves, the terror-filled joy of lighting fuses, the sulfur smell on the cold air, your now-dead parents' voices, sober and cautionary early-evening, alcohol-fueled and animated as they joined you outside at midnight.

What you wouldn't know is that as the paddleboat turned to head downriver at Redbud Island, where in September they found our flood-lost Natalie, one of Mark Soto's bottle rockets, as if to make up for the miracle of the iguana, will misfire, sputter onto his roof, and into the leaf-cluttered rain gutter. Dry wood shingles. A cold stiff wind. Up it will go. His parents out celebrating at a New Year's party. The teenage sister inside the house making out with her boyfriend, the music up. Mark will try to put the fire out with the garden hose. Before he can even call the fire department—which he'll wait too long to do out of fear—it will be fully engaged. Eventually smelling the smoke, the sister, still buttoning up her blouse, will lope outside with the boyfriend. When Mark Soto's parents drive up, they'll find the bones of their house aglow like an X-ray, fire trucks, and hoses snaking through the street. Water rushing. Their son Mark will be sitting hands-between-knees on Dennis and Winnie's curb, his face bright with the flames, beside him his round-eyed sister, the boyfriend long gone. And stacked on the sidewalk, a few meager possessions rescued from their garage: an orange hamster cage, a shoebox of photos, and, staring out from the terrarium, the iguana, unblinking, inscrutable as the Buddha.

32

At midnight, P.G. kissed Melinda to celebrate the new millennium, the real one, he told her, that respected proper numerical beginnings and ends, not the false prophet of 2000. He was about to explain how, in medieval times, they had a numeric basis for apocalypse, when Melinda asked if he wanted to fuck or talk numbers all night. Their sex life had improved dramatically the last month or so. Sometimes he even let Melinda wear the brocade vest, though guilt would often seize him and his tooth would ache as if he'd bitten down on a pebble.

After they'd made love and Melinda had fallen asleep, P.G. went to meet his middleman, Howard Brakhage, at Deep Eddy Cabaret. A couple of detectives had stopped by Howard's autobody shop on South 1st the week before to ask him questions. "Shamuses," Howard said. He nodded, significantly, sipped his beer.

P.G. looked at him. Howard's statements were often aphoristic, a kind of noir-speak that drove P.G. crazy. Howard was a big fan of Raymond Chandler novels and detective movies. Howard did have a way with language, P.G. would give him that. He'd taught himself Italian while in the Marines by watching Italian porno movies. He would say something simple and crude like "your husband has a limp sardine" in Italian and it would sound beautiful, like water lapping at a shore.

"Shamuses?" P.G. said, looking at him dumbly.

Around them, overdressed people coming from

somewhere else huddled at beer bottle-cluttered tables. In the middle of each table, a paper rose stuck from a plastic vase. The Stones' "Tumbling Dice" played on the jukebox.

"Shamuses," Howard said. "You know." Again, the significant look.

"Dumb it down a little for me, Howard," P.G. said. "I'm a literalist."

Howard leaned forward, spoke close to P.G.'s ear. "Homicide detectives, okay?" Howard glanced over at the table next to them, looked back at P.G.

P.G. grinned.

"At least I try to have some kind of decorum," Howard said. "Christ."

P.G. said he was sorry. Drank down his beer, walked up to the bar and ordered another for himself and Howard. He thought of the old man, leaning against the tree. The hole in his throat. P.G. wondered if he'd gone to the police. His tooth began to throb. When he got back to the table, he asked Howard what questions the detectives had. Howard said they showed him some photos of SUV's and a few Toyota 4x4 trucks. They asked him if he kept track of makes and models and the kinds of repair work he'd done back in September. Howard told them he would have to get back to them. "They wouldn't tell me what it was about," Howard said. He was quiet for a few seconds, ate a handful of peanuts. "Have any idea?" he asked.

"Not a clue," P.G. said. He would need to get rid of some computer hard drives, shred some documents. The detectives might be back with a warrant.

Howard pulled the paper rose from the vase, put it to his nose. "Do you like orchids?" he said in an aristocratic voice, slipping into his *Big Sleep* routine.

P.G. went along. "Not particularly," P.G. said in a half-hearted Bogart.

"Nasty things," Howard said. "Their flesh is too much like the flesh of men, and their perfume has the rotten sweetness of corruption."

"Not bad," P.G. said. "Your cadence was a little off, though."

Howard picked at his beer label. He complimented P.G. on the brocade vest. "Has some style," he said.

P.G. dipped his head in an exaggerated bow. Smiled.

A woman at the bar shouted that everybody should be dancing. She knocked her beer bottle to the floor and it shattered. People cheered.

"Happy New Year, by the way," Howard said, grudgingly.

"New millennium," P.G. said. He clinked beers with Howard. "2000 was just a marketing ploy."

"Well, I don't feel any difference. You feel any difference?" Howard was always talking about getting out of the auto body shop business, about how his life had come to a standstill.

"Yessir, I do," P.G. said. "I feel like I'm being swept along to somewhere good. It's hard to explain. But it's like a current has me and pretty soon I'll be worlds away."

"*Siete nell'amore con il destino*," Howard said in his Italian.

"Absolutely," P.G. said, knowing these were the right words even if he couldn't understand them.

* * *

Driving home from the bar, P.G. saw the glow of the fire. When he turned down Meriden Street, neighbors were out in their yards bundled in robes and jackets. Fire trucks. Police cars. The air pulsed with light. He parked, got out, walked up the street. Flames leaped from the roof of 701 Meriden. High-up tree limbs had caught fire. They looked to P.G. like burning arteries. He could feel the heat against his face. The air smelled like burned plastic. Firefighters were wetting down the roofs of surrounding houses. He saw Bob Patterson, whom he'd recently sold a flood-zone policy to. Dennis Lipsy and his son. A bundled pregnant woman he didn't recognize. He asked Dennis if there was anything he could do and Dennis said no, they were going to call a neighborhood meeting and pass the hat for the Sotos, see about getting them somewhere to stay. P.G. said maybe he could help out on that end. In one of the neighboring driveways, Henry Soto was consoling his wife. Winnie Lipsy was there, too. P.G. wasn't more than five feet away from offering his sympathies, when he glimpsed the old man standing at the edge of the trees near the greenbelt entrance.

***

P.G. shuffled sideways down the side of the hill and through a thick strand of bamboo. The fire lit up parts of the creek like an arc light, threw other parts into shadow. Water gurgled in the creek. *I knew who it would be*, the old man had said. P.G. heard something move in the brush. He plunged into bunch grass and thistle. From across the creek bed, a large buck stared back at him. Eyes shining. The buck made a coughing sound and bounded off. P.G. crossed the creek, scrambled up a limestone ledge, making an X with his body over a crevice. He was breathing hard. Acrid smoke caught in his throat. He pulled himself up and over the edge of the bluff, not even sure where he was. In a space through the branches he could see stars and drifting dark patches he supposed were smoke. Something rustled. "Anyone there?" he called. No answer. He kept going. In front of him, poking awkwardly from the bank, was the shoe tree. Farther on, through scrub oak and cedar, he could see house lights. A fence of some kind. A gate. He kept walking. The back of the house came into view, wooden deck, sun room, large high windows. Framed in one of the windows was a woman carefully taping shut a box. Her hair pulled up in a bandana.

The dog came out of nowhere. Thumping along the ground, then a snarling explosion against the chain link fence. P.G. had been in the yard, he supposed, when he'd heard the dog coming. Now he stood outside it again, though he couldn't remember how he'd gotten back over the fence.

A floodlight came on. A door opened. "Harry?" the woman called from the porch. "Harry? Get back here," she said. "Leave the deer alone. You are such a dumbass." Harry kept barking. P.G. could see now that the woman in the porch light was Charlotte Branch. She walked towards him. P.G. stood perfectly still. Pain shot through his jaw. There were some low hanging cedars in front of his face. He was standing just outside the arc of the floodlight.

Harry kept on.

"What am I going to do with you?" Charlotte Branch said.

Standing a half-dozen feet away, his heart stuttering, P.G. thought he caught a kind of sad music in her voice.

VI

33

I've lost my wedding ring, Odie says, staring at the back of his hand. I'm sure it was there a minute ago.

Well, don't look at me, Jones says. He glances down the creek bed. Maybe the girl needed it. For her intended.

Ruth will be upset, Odie says.

Trust is what makes a relationship, Odie.

People always say that when they want something, Odie says.

Odie, I read in the newspaper about this guide who took people on helicopter sightseeing trips over the Grand Canyon. The guide would point out the millions of years of strata the water had exposed down there. Beautiful redwall limestone, wine-dark hermit shale. Anyway, one day, the guide was explaining away like this when the fella next to him suddenly takes off his wedding ring and hands it to the guide. Takes off his watch, hands that to the woman in the seat next to him. Before anyone can say anything, he unlatches his seatbelt, gets up, opens the copter door and leaps out. No give my love to Rose. No Geronimo. Nothing. Just out and down. He leaves the others behind to tell the story.

But they can't tell his story. They can only tell their own.

When I think of that fella, I always picture Wile E. Coyote paused there in midair for a second or so.

But it's not the end, Odie says. Odie rubs his finger where the wedding ring had been. The story keeps going: The helicopter lands, Odie says. The guide is in shock. He gives his statement to the police, forgets all about the wedding ring in his pocket until the lady with the watch says something. He goes home and dreams about the leaping man, feels himself grabbing for him but only grasping air, sees the leaping man growing smaller and smaller until he's a speck below in the canyon. The guide can't eat his dinner, can't make love to his wife. Pretty soon, he discovers he can't look at his maps the same way anymore either, can't even mention outloud some of the familiar names of the canyon topography. He develops an ulcer and quits giving tours. Soon, he's broke. His wife is unhappy. He's changed, she says. Why can't he get on with things? He doesn't know.

I hope there aren't any teeth in this story, Jones says. He grins.

Eventually, Odie says, his wife leaves him. He's alone, except for the leaping man in his head. After knocking around several jobs, he sets about becoming a Pentecostal minister. He builds his church upon the rock, on the certainty of God's plan. He dedicates his life to making His purposes plain. But he loses faith. There are indiscretions. His church is investigated for accounting fraud. He's defrocked or what have you. He's in despair. Even thinks about killing himself.

Happens to the best of us, Jones says.

Then, for some reason, he finds himself drawn back to the canyon. He takes a job mending hiking boots in the gear rental shop at first, then starts to lead hikes down to the river. He mouths the familiar names of places again. Looks up at the same rock strata he used to look down on. He won't ever be over it, the man decides. He is changed—irrevocably so—though he can't be certain in what ways. He notices small things he hadn't noticed here before: The avalanches of little stones bighorn sheep send down. The popping sound sandstone makes as it cools and contracts at night. He wonders if somehow the leaping man's enthusiasm for the ground has become part of him. He goes on. The story doesn't end where you say.

A stick in the river, Jones says. A tock to his tick.

You were dying.

They died for me, Odie.

You didn't have the courage to put an end to it. Before it started.

You don't know what you're talking about. You're malnourished, Odie. Eating all those roots and acorns. Dumpster diving. Not enough oxygen to the brain.

You were eating a melon when I found you, Odie says. The children I was supposed to innoculate, still in their mothers' embrace. Flies on their faces.

Help us to the ending we deserve, Odie. We are weary. Round and round we go.

The end is a sleight of hand, Odie says. A look here so you don't see there. I remember now.

How could you remember? You can't even keep straight who died for whom.

You waited for me.

Any old someone would have done the trick.

You put the gun to your head.

Jones makes a gun of his cigar, points it at his own head. It smolders there.

You hesitated. Lost your nerve. Your hand was shaking.

Jones sighs. At least any old someone would have remembered what actually happened. Would have given us the ending we deserved.

I grabbed your arm.

You were supposed to tell the story, not be in it. What

about your Hippocratic oath?

The gun went off.

Do you know what it's like to hear a whistle and realize it's the wind blowing through a hole in your face? Jones looks at Odie's throat. Oh, he says. Sorry. I forgot.

You were still breathing, lying there, Odie says.

The weary old contingent world wobbles on like a bad tire. Do no harm, they say, but how can you not?

You begged me to kill you, Odie says. I picked up the gun off the floor. I pulled the trigger.

Words fail, Odie.

Not always.

You had malice in your heart, Jones says. Who could blame you? All those little ones, dead?

I had pity in my heart, Odie says. The bullet loves the wound that begot it.

34

"What hurts most is that I wasn't there with her," Charlotte Branch told P.G. They were standing in Charlotte's kitchen the week after he'd hidden in the trees behind her fence. The last few moving boxes squatted on the counters and floor. He'd opened his insurance case on the breakfast bar between two of the boxes, but hadn't yet gotten into details about payouts or policy changes. He could smell a garlic seafood dish—stuffed shrimp? scallops?—she'd cooked for dinner. Could almost taste the butter on his tongue.

P.G. said he understood. He had a boy of his own now and knew he'd lay down his life for him if it came to it. "I doubt if I could have imagined that a year ago," he said. He saw his son a year from now, a red balloon tied by a string to his toddler finger. The balloon wobbles up, the string grows taut. His son laughs, scrunches his nose.

There was a long silence. The water heater gurgled from the utility room. Charlotte's face was thin, gnawed on, he supposed, by sleeplessness and intruders like himself. Near the door, he'd seen boxes with Natalie's things, black-markered lists on their tops. Computer software. Books.

"So," P.G. said. "I know this isn't the best time to approach you about this, Mrs. Branch, but what often happens is that the beneficiary will roll over the cash from the deceased's policy into an IRA account for safe-keeping. A tidy nest egg that—

"—Nest egg?" Charlotte Branch said, a bemused look on her face, as if she saw the image but couldn't make heads or tails. She gathered a stack of Tupperware from a drawer and put it inside a box.

"A poor choice of words on my part," P.G. said. He felt failure again settle into his legs. He stared at his gleaming black case on the counter. Why was he here?

"It's all right," Charlotte said. "I'm not offended. It's just a figure of speech."

"Still," P.G. said. "I wonder sometimes if I've been at this too long. Saying things like that."

"You're doing fine," she said. She turned back to the boxes, taped one flap down.

"I'm intruding on you," P.G. said.

"No. I'm just distracted." She looked at him. "The movers come tomorrow." She piled her milk-coffee hair on her head and re-clipped it. "Your voice keeps me from listening to a big empty house. Very loud, really, in all its quiet. It's funny." She smiled.

Out in the backyard, Harry the dog howled along with a siren.

P.G. saw Natalie again in the roiling water, her leg twined in roots.

P.G. stood over his black case, fingered some file folders, closed its lid. He told Charlotte Branch he was very sorry but he had to leave, he just remembered that his wife had a La Leche League meeting. He grabbed the case, headed toward the side door, caught his foot on a box, but steadied himself before he fell. His extremities felt numb. The tooth had started up again. The dog kept howling.

Charlotte was watching him.

He looked at Charlotte's hand on the box flap. "I stayed with her," P.G. heard himself say, calmly, as if speaking to someone on the other side of the breakfast bar about a movie they might see.

***

He'd failed, somehow. Charlotte hadn't understood. They'd sat together in the living room on her cellophane-wrapped couch. He'd watched her jaw harden, her eyes burn with the recognition of what he was saying. A flicker, then it was out. He'd failed. He had tried to explain. About the Blazer, about how he'd found her. About swift water rising. Natalie's breath against his cheek. But Charlotte had gotten it mixed up. "You heard the tires squeal and knew there'd been an accident?" she'd said. She stared at him, her face rigid, waiting.

"I knew," he said.

"You stayed with her?"

"Yes. Down in the creek bed."

"You spoke softly to her, held her hand?"

"To soothe her."

"Promised her you wouldn't leave?" Charlotte looked around the living room: moving boxes to bookcase to dry cleaning hanging on the closet door.

"I promised," P.G. said. He ran his fingers along the satin of the vest. He couldn't feel his legs, as if blood had stopped circulating there.

With one hand, Charlotte gripped his rolled shirtsleeve and it seemed to P.G. that without her holding him he would have fallen sideways. They sat together as the living room windows darkened, until finally there was no more for P.G. to tell.

35

And then it was March and we opened our windows to incandescent blue sky and heard again along our streets the tacka-tack of skateboards off curbs, the earnest, discordant notes from our children's trumpets and guitars. During the afternoon, jackhammers and backhoes dug up the guts of the access road. Access to what? We wondered, idling in jaw-clenched traffic at rush hour, only a half-mile from our homes. Telecommunications, *the City said when we called.* Fiber optics. The wired world. *But we'd stare at the gaping holes, piled dirt and crumbled asphalt and think absently of Odie's many surgeries and extractions, the severing of muscle, ligament, bone.*

At night, we'd hear the train headed south along the Loop. It would then turn east to cross the river, its wail dropping several octaves like a rebuke.

***

We came and went: transfers, layoffs, bankruptcies, foreclosures, marriages, divorces. We put houses up for sale and tore decrepit ones down. Had bitter disputes over property lines and zoning. Envied one another to the point of distraction, attended baby showers and parties, visited hospital rooms after tonsillectomies, and helped raise one another's children with a mixture of enmity and love.

We kept going.

***

In April we had a festival in our park, not so much to celebrate spring, as to stave off the heat-hammered summer. Our children dressed up as Eeyores and Captain Hooks and Ariels. A salsa band played. We drank beer, joined in three-legged races, lurched and lunged to ground or finish line. Our eyes drawn every so often to the creek bed where the shoe tree poked from the rocky shoal.

The sun settled into the trees and we paced off our steps and readied our hands. And then Odie appeared in the middle of the field, stood transfixed, as the eggs, hundreds of them, arced through the dimming sky. Our hands cradled some, fumbled others. Shrieks of laughter. Broken shells scattered on the grass. A few of us moved through the crowd toward Odie, children in face paint bumping our thighs. But when we got there, he was gone.

From the stage, conga drums raced feverishly, then slowed. Trumpets blared. Dennis thought he saw Odie near the Maypole, barefoot, pants legs rolled, calmly eating a turkey leg. But when the song finished, he found himself staring at a Hispanic man in running shorts.

When darkness fell, the fire jugglers lit their batons and the crowd clapped wildly. The congas started up their thumping again. We milled about in the flickering shadows. The park police barked through a bullhorn that the park was closing, to grab your things. The crowd shouted back drunkenly, but moved in ragged unison toward the park entrance. The congas kept on, gained momentum, indifferent to what was at hand. And just before the power was shut off and the world leaped into murmuring darkness, we saw Odie once more, being swept toward the entrance, his silver-haired head bobbing in the crowd, eyes fixed on the jungle canopy overhead.

36

"Taking care of crazy old people becomes you," Margo Farbrother said to Dennis in the car. Her arms were still smooth and sinewy. Her hair, shorter now, streaked with gray like her father's used to be. Her nose flatter than Dennis remembered.

"It's all part of my get-rich-quick scheme," Dennis said.

He'd picked up Margo at her hotel. They were driving out west of town, on Highway 290, toward Dripping Springs, to check on Sonny. The sun was beginning to sink behind the hills. Dennis had missed the turnoff for the zoo, the only real marker along the way to Sonny's place, and had had to double back. He needed to be home by 8:30 that night for Isaac's birthday dinner. They were having the recently displaced Sotos over.

"And here all this time I thought Sonny was spending his money on whores and cocaine," Margo said.

"Don't put it past him," Dennis said.

"No," Margo said. "I'd never put anything past him." She smiled but it made Dennis want to look back at the road.

On the phone earlier, Margo had told Dennis she hadn't been able to reach Sonny all day, that lately, his cedar allergies had worsened his emphysema. Half the time, Margo had said, he didn't take his medication and the other half he took too much and got depressed. Dennis knew she must be worried, too, about her place in all this. Why she was even here to begin with, given her and Sonny's history. Margo had told Dennis on the phone that since her mom died, she'd had to rethink things. "But rethinking something doesn't necessarily mean changing your mind about it," Margo had said. She hadn't elaborated. Dennis hadn't pushed. Margo had been in town off and on since December when Sonny had gone in the hospital with pneumonia. The guardianship case would be decided in a few weeks, but Dennis still held out hope Sonny would simply give in.

Next to him in the car, Margo said, "So why isn't he answering his phone, you think?" She chewed her lip.

"Don't know. Just stubborn, probably," Dennis said.

"He thinks I'm trying to punish him," Margo said. She crossed her arms, looked off at billboards selling Hill Country real estate.

"I think it's crossed his mind," Dennis said.

"He's been out of my life for a long time," she said, absently.

"Yes," he said. "He has." In Dennis's head, he saw Sonny's arm sling a handful of gravel.

"You're a dad, right?" Her voice brightened.

"I am. A boy. Isaac. He's about to turn nine." Dennis decided not to mention the birthday dinner.

"I bet he looks like you. Same dimples."

"A little like both of us, I guess," Dennis said. He grabbed his wallet from the console, opened it to a photo of Isaac, Winnie, and himself. She took the photo out, held it up. "He's a cutie," she said. She pressed the photo to her forehead, like a carnival fortune-teller. "And your wife's name is Winnie," she said in a theatrical voice. She smiled. "I did a search on the internet earlier," she said. "She's lovely, isn't she? Hazel eyes." It struck Dennis that Margo was piecing him together in her head.

"She's a pediatric nurse," Dennis said. "Neonatology."

"Babies," Margo said, with a kind of helpless awe, as if

she saw rows of them laid out before her.

"It's a tough job," Dennis said. "Babies with diseases. Don't think I could handle it."

"I bet you're a good dad," Margo said.

The image of Isaac tumbling from the tree came to him. "Sometimes I wonder," he said.

She narrowed her eyes at him. "You ever certain about anything?" Then she smiled.

"How about you? Ever married?"

"Was. A pilot for Delta. In my early-twenties. He was, well, older. Things got dicey pretty quick. I used to dream he'd be passing over our house and he'd fling my luggage out and I'd find my clothes all exploded up in the trees."

"Some dream," Dennis said. He saw Margo's clothes fluttering in the branches. "Any kids?"

"Can't have them," Margo said. "Endometriosis." She looked out the window at the scrub cedars. "No more Farbrothers," she said, tracing her finger through the window condensation. It was turning cooler. Then she looked at Dennis. "Not the worst thing that could happen, I guess," she said.

Dennis thought of the night of the party, years ago, Margo's story, Sonny's mouth full of feathers. *Come on down and give me a kiss*. He wondered how you got over something like that, if you ever did. *You can't change what's coming by being one place or the other,* she'd said. But here she was. What did she want from Sonny? What could Sonny give?

"There are probably just as many reasons not to have kids as to have them," Dennis said.

"Not for you—you've got every reason in the world," she said.

They were quiet for a few seconds. Around them, the hills were purple and gold. He couldn't look at her. What was he thinking saying something like that? As if she had a choice. He fiddled with the radio but the station was fading. Finally, Dennis said, "Isaac's a funny kid." Then, he remembered a story about Isaac that he'd nearly forgotten. The clarity of it surprised him. He looked over at Margo, who was staring out at the hills. "When Isaac was little, maybe five or so, there was this solar eclipse," he said. "I told Isaac not to stare at it. Told him it would hurt his eyes if he did. That people burned their retinas that way, went blind that way. But I didn't know how literal kids take things. Turns out he ended up peddling his Big Wheel the whole day with his head down, afraid he'd catch an eyeful. Only, I didn't know this. I was at work. In the evening, when I got home, he was quiet. Stuck to himself. Watched some TV. Finally, around bedtime, he came up to me. 'Dad,' he said, 'I saw it.' Just like that. Solemn. 'I saw it.' He wanted to know when he would be blinded. I tried to explain he wouldn't, that you have to stare steady and long, but it took a good while to convince him otherwise. He's a funny kid."

"Not a doubting Thomas like you. The kid has conviction." Dennis could feel Margo's eyes on him.

"I guess that's one way to look at it," he said. He smiled but she didn't smile back. He thought of Isaac's pinched mouth that time. Afraid to tell because maybe telling would make it come true.

Dennis turned off the highway and onto the dirt road to Sonny's place. They wound down between limestone bluffs until they came to a low water crossing at the creek. The water was shadowy in the falling light. Above them, along the top of the bluff, the last of the sun burned. They were quiet again. And for some reason, maybe the strange light, he thought of Natalie sitting up on her lifeguard chair at the pool, her face shaded by her wide-brimmed hat. But when he tried to picture her face, he couldn't. Instead, he saw Winnie's face from the photo. Her wide-set eyes. He thought of two mornings ago, when he woke around 4:00 and found her awake beside him. He'd asked her if she wanted to talk. About Allison. About them. But she said that she couldn't find the words right now. Three weeks before, at the end of February, Allison had gone back to Alaska, back to her boyfriend, Zach. She and Winnie had had fights near the end. Winnie had insisted on having a new family portrait made, though Dennis had tried to talk her out of it. Allison had asked why Winnie hadn't shown up the first time around. The last few days before catching the bus back, Allison had checked into the youth hostel over on Riverside Drive. She would have the baby in a week or so, he imagined.

Sonny's stone house rose at the top of the hill. Goats grazed here and there. Sonny's pickup was parked on the side of the house.

Dennis pulled the car up the gravel drive and they got out, walked up to the house. From the porch, they could hear the water rushing in the creek below. "Seems like a hundred years since I've been here," Margo said. "But then it doesn't seem a day."

Dennis heard a low rumbling echo off the bluffs that made the hair on the back of his neck stand up, though he knew what it was.

"What the hell's that?" Margo said.

"The lions, over at the zoo," Dennis said. Sonny had told him about them roaring at feeding times. How he'd sit on his porch in the evening in the spring, waiting for them to start. A low, alive sound you first felt on your insides. "Oh that's nothing," Sonny had said to him. "You should hear them fucking."

"Wow," Margo said, staring off at the bluffs. "I bet the

goats piss themselves."

After knocking on the front door, they went to the side of the house and Dennis looked in one of the larger windows. A lamp shone on the desk. Newspapers and magazines were piled all around. Then, on the floor, sticking out beside the couch, Dennis saw Sonny's brown work boots, jean cuffs. Dennis's mouth went dry. He didn't say anything to Margo. The window was unlocked so he raised it and heaved himself inside, half-expecting the smell of Sonny's decomposing body to hit him. Instead, the air was stale. Cigarette smoke. Mildew.

He told Margo to wait at the window. "Why?" She asked in a small voice, but nodded as if she already knew the answer. Her eyes were rounded and shiny.

When Dennis got to him, Sonny was lying on his stomach on the floor, legs apart. Dennis bent down to take his pulse. That's when Sonny raised up onto his knees, laughing. Then a coughing spasm seized him. He finally caught his breath, got up off the floor. He eyed Margo warily at the window. Turned to Dennis, clapped him on the shoulder. "You were thinking: now that son-of-a-bitch is either dead or my watch has stopped."

***

After he got home, Dennis stood in the dark behind the wooden trellis he'd put up last year for Winnie's trumpet vine. Some of the perennials in the flowerbed were coming back. He could hear the tick of his cooling engine. Across the street, the Pattersons' automated sprinklers started. The cool spring nights would end soon. Summer would press in. Dennis could see, between the trellis slats, Henry and Mercedes Soto in his bay window, sitting at the dining table. Beside them, their daughter and their son, Mark, who had burned down their house. They'd moved into an apartment across town nearly three months ago. Two houses away from where they sat, squatted the blackened ruin of their house, yet here they were. In the bay window, they seemed to Dennis like any family you might meet: full of the same faults and long stares, teetering there on the edge of their future, one they couldn't guess at. And watching them at the table, smiling, teasing one another, Dennis could imagine them welcoming it. With all its blind chance and back-sliding. With all its contradictions. They welcomed it. It was as if they knew their lives by feel, the way you'd know a familiar room even in the dark. Know the space between where the bed ends and the hallway begins.

In the window, Isaac, the birthday boy, laughed at something Henry Soto was saying. Winnie was leaning on one elbow, smiling, her other hand flying to her mouth the way it did. Her smile startled him. It seemed wistful but not entirely sad. As if some feeling that had been shaping her all along was gone and she was just beginning to miss it.

Dennis walked across the lawn and into the porch light and Winnie looked up and saw him. Her face grew animated. She pointed him out to the others. Walked to the window, waved him inside.

* * *

"I like the sound of people in our house," Isaac told Dennis. Isaac was helping Dennis clear the dining table after the Sotos left. It was late.

Dennis said, "Well, *we're* people. *We* make sounds." He grinned at Isaac. Sipped his bourbon. *Twine Time*, a local R&B show, was on the radio. William Bell sang "You Don't Miss Your Water." Through the kitchen doorway, Dennis could see Winnie rinsing dishes at the sink, swaying a little to the music, one stocking foot to the other. Her hair was up. She was wearing a dark green dress with spaghetti straps and he could see the pale skin of her neck and shoulders. She turned, stood on her toes to put a serving dish in a high-up cabinet. She caught him looking at her. She leaned back against the sink, arms crossed. Stared back at him, an appraisal. What did she see?

She stuck the tip of her tongue out at him like a cat.

"I don't mean us," Isaac told Dennis in a frustrated voice. He stared at a wadded up linen napkin on the table. "You made it into a joke."

Dennis cleared his throat. "I didn't mean to," he said. "I'm sorry." It occurred to him he and Winnie hadn't prepared Isaac for what might happen. With Allison. With the baby. Wasn't that what parents were supposed to do, prepare for contingencies? Have foresight? "I know you liked having Allison here," Dennis said.

Isaac nodded, grudgingly. Gathered up a fistful of silverware and seemed to think something over, then he said, "Maybe we can we have a birthday dinner for the baby."

Dennis looked at him. "Sure. We could do that," he said. He stacked dessert plates, gathered coffee cups.

"Why did she leave?"

Dennis said, "I think she missed things. Back in Alaska."

Isaac thought about this for a second. "I guess her home is in Alaska," he said matter-of-factly.

"Right," Dennis said. "She wanted to go home."

"Do you think she'll miss us?"

Through the dining room window, Dennis could see the moon shining on the roofs of cars parked along their street. "I think she already does," Dennis said. He saw Allison on the boat in the photo she'd sent them, her eyes darting outside the frame.

She had come for a beginning, he supposed, some kind of explanation. But Winnie couldn't give it to her, though she'd tried. Only dates and places and names: the unfelt facts of a life. What was there to stitch them together?

"Dad, are you sleepy?" Isaac asked.

"A little."

"I am too. A little," Isaac said.

"It was a big day," Dennis said. He ran his hand through Isaac's hair, which was getting wavy as he got older, turning darker. A mix of his own and Winnie's.

Issac seemed to drift off again. Then he asked, "Dad, do babies sleep a lot, inside their mothers?"

"They do, almost all the time," Dennis said.

"I guess that's how they get ready," Isaac said.

"I think that's right," Dennis said.

"They dream about it, too, probably. About what's coming." Isaac's eyes narrowed.

"Maybe so," Dennis said. "Maybe they dream of the people who will take care of them."

Isaac seemed to think this over, then walked into the living room, picked up the radio-controlled plane the Sotos had given him off the coffee table. He passed the plane through the air, swooped low with it, over magazines and highball glasses on the coffee table. After awhile, he curled up on the couch, the airplane still in his hand. When Dennis looked over again, he was asleep.

A little later, after they finished cleaning up and putting Isaac to bed, Dennis pulled the sleeping bags from the hall closet, brought them out on their darkened porch. Winnie opened the porch windows, so they could hear the radio. Sometimes, too, Isaac would call out for them after a bad dream. Damp, cool air had settled in. They hung the hammock between the posts, tossed the bags in, and crawled inside. They hadn't been in the hammock since the summer before. "Bundled up like Bedouins," Winnie said in her sing-songy drunk voice. Dennis thought of Joseph's coat of many colors. Something like a jester's outfit, he supposed. Joseph had prophetic dreams. When Joseph told his brothers about the dreams, they tried to kill him. Someone stuck him down a well. And then he got out. But Dennis couldn't remember how. "Your hands are cold," Winnie said. She rubbed them between her own. On the radio, they listened to James Brown sing "Please, Please, Please" and "Try Me." Told stories about the first time they'd heard particular songs. What they were doing. Who they were with. There were spaces between what they said and did, Dennis knew. Mutual disappointments that made their bodies stutter and seem strange. Even now, as they undressed in the sleeping bag, the hammock swaying under them. They kissed. Tentatively, at first. Eyelids. Lips. Fingers. They felt along. Fumbled. Remembered by touch things they'd forgotten. Winnie's small hand clasped the back of his shoulder. "Scapula," she said, absently. "That's what this bony ridge is." Then Dennis felt her hand splayed there, as if taking the measure of something. The familiar fit of it.

They made love, silently. Fell asleep to the late night radio host's steady mumble.

Later, Dennis woke up to the ringing of his cell phone. It was in his pants pocket and he had to fumble below on the porch to find it. Change fell from his pants. "Hello?" he said, finally, into the phone, panic and irritation edging in. "Who is this?" He could hear breathing. He didn't recognize the number shown on the phone. Some drunk-dialing college kid, he imagined. He was about to hang up, when the image of Sonny came to him, chain-smoking, pacing his dark porch. Blood thrummed in Dennis's ears. "Sonny?" he said, finally. "Is that you?" Nothing. His thoughts tumbled. He saw Odie slumped inside a phone booth somewhere. Then, on the phone, there was an exhale, as if whoever it was had been holding his breath a long time. Not a sound of frustration or impatience. It just sounded natural, he thought, as if someone had been underwater and had just come up for air. "It's late," Dennis said gently into the phone. "Is there something you need? Something I can help you with?" It had gotten cold. The sky was clear. The moon low. Across the street, he could see a cluster of stars above the Pattersons' roofline. He felt his bare leg against Winnie in the sleeping bag, the warmth of her thigh.

There was a loud rustling on the phone. "I'm here," Dennis said.

37

Natalie knows she is in the creek bed where the truck threw her. Still, it seems a mistake, a slip of the tongue that might be brought back. Regret twists inside her. She fingers her lifeguard whistle, its twining cord. *The pool is closing*, she thinks. *But the sunset is in the wrong place.* She wonders if the stock film footage has been mixed up. She whistles the last swimmers from the pool anyway. Towels-over-shoulders, they head toward the exit. Some of her swim students peel off from parents to hug her goodbye. Next year, they say excitedly, we will be sand sharks or manta rays or marlins. Their eyes shine. She loves them and would dream them up if they didn't exist. With the dip net she fishes out their hair bands, candy wrappers, and left-behind goggles from the pool bottom. But when she looks again, she sees wedding rings, watches, ankle bracelets, medical ID tags. Frustration rises in her throat. She wants to say something to the swimmers about their negligence, but knows they are long gone.

From the entrance, Griff, the pool manager, whom the summer-before she had loved beyond reason, yells, *lights!* and for a few seconds there is flickering above the pool like heat lightning and then they go out. In the dark, something whirs to life, and for a second Natalie thinks of Amaranta's sewing machine. Amaranta's sisters' fingers singing like crickets. But she sees the glow of the projector and realizes she's forgotten it's movie night at the pool. Someone takes her hand. Her movie date? She can't quite make out his face but knows he's meant for her. Below the grass berm, where half the neighborhood sits on blankets under the creaking cottonwoods, a screen is lit up with images that at first make no sense. But then Natalie sees it's a movie about her. Imagine someone going to all that trouble, she thinks. Saving film footage of the smallest gestures. Her dad squatting on his bad knees, tenderly smoothing her forehead after she'd run headlong into the picnic table, her mother timidly linking an arm in her dad's for a photo that first Christmas after their separation, Natalie holding Dennis's trembling hand against her face in the kitchen that time. Then some smart-ass kid is standing in front of the screen, making shadow animals with his hands. The crowd jeers or cheers, she can't tell which. The wind picks up. The cottonwood leaves roar.

Then, as if the projector has turned on her, it's noontime-bright. She sees the smart-ass kid, one of the deaf boys from the State School who visits the pool the second Tuesday of every month, has fallen in. He's flailing his arms above the water like they're on fire. His eyes are half-dollars in his head. Then he goes down. Natalie is into the water and over to him, quick. She tries to get a grip on him, but he fights her. Climbs her body. Pulls at her hair. They're knotted together. She twists around and swings an arm under both of his, then kicks for the side. The boy must weigh next to nothing but in the water he's dense, like one of the old cypress logs people find on the river bottom. He wants to slip away but she won't let him. She thinks how the body's words are movements, the way a hand cups the water like so, and then pulls it behind like so, forgetting itself in doing, but the head fools you with words like love and fear and always, words that angle away from where you want them to go.

She concentrates on her strokes.

Near the edge of the pool, someone grabs the boy from her, heaves him out. When Natalie climbs up the ladder, he's lying in the grass. Her wide-brimmed hat is beside him. A group of deaf school kids and a few other lifeguards gather around. Mrs. Rosenberg, who swam everyday at the pool for her sciatica, but who died months ago, is there, too, hand to mouth with concern.

The boy eases up on his side, retches up a rope of water and bile onto the grass. He wipes his mouth and sits up cautiously. He looks around, tight-lipped, and begins signing furiously. One of the older deaf boys says he's asking for his mother. Griff calls an ambulance. People come over to thank Natalie. Her movie date, looking out of place in a suit, waves shyly, shifting on his feet. Dennis touches her elbow. *You okay?* he asks. His face opens to her, a fist unclenching. What's there? Desire? Pity? Love? Filled up with all three, she decides. Here's the church, here's the steeple, open the doors and there's all the people. She touches her arm where Dennis touched, and her hand comes away with a smear of blood. Teeth marks purple the flesh. *A real fighter*, Dennis says. Winnie is there, too, her eyes darting around for Isaac in the deep end. Natalie sees something in Winnie's face that's drowning and wants to climb onto Natalie to be saved. Natalie puts out her hand.

The boy begins to cry. His knotted up face and trembling lips remind Natalie of a baby's. She feels a sudden pressure in her uterus and wonders if she'll have kids. She once saw a PBS show in which a woman delivered a baby underwater. More like where they come from, she thinks.

She sits cross-legged in the grass. The EMT crew is there suddenly, working on the boy. *How many fingers?* One asks. But he's missing several of his own.

Then the sun is going down again.

She lets it go.

Across the river, at the canoe rental shop, the blue pier

lights come on. The sky is water, the land water. *The magic hour, again*, she thinks. A whole day come and gone.

The deaf boy rises naked from the stretcher. He's younger now, maybe two or so. His skin is ruddy as if he has a rash. He staggers like a drunk over to the pool edge and everyone smiles. Then he pees into the water to great applause. When he's finished, he waddles over to her, curls up in her lap. He tugs at her swimsuit until he can reach her breast. Everything grows small until there is only the burning circle of his mouth on her. His eyes grateful and clear. His hands opening and closing.

All around them, dozens of his school friends squat in the shadowy grass and begin to sign. Softly, softly, they rasp out words from their bodies, like insects at night.

38

And then, as in one of our dreams, Odie came back.

Ruth was out walking on the greenbelt as she did every afternoon now. On the way home, she smelled curry in the air. She grew suddenly hungry. Ravenous, she would tell us later. When she passed Dennis and Winnie's house, she tasted the pulpy flesh of mangoes. Darnell Greer pulled alongside Ruth in his pickup, told her about the macaws getting out of their cages, the ruckus they were raising in the trees. Ruth stared at him uncomprehendingly. She never paused. She walked on. She passed the Branch's, where a broken sprinkler head geysered water into the trees. Turned left on 7th, crossed the creek, headed up the walk and into her own house. From the entryway, she could see the sliding glass door ajar in the kitchen. The ceiling fan turning in the living room. Newspaper scattered on the floor. Then, poking from the recliner, the back of Odie's silver head.

She made her way into the room, studied his ravaged, sun-mottled face and at first felt nothing, she would tell Winnie later. Her life stalled so long she'd nearly forgotten the groove it ran in.

We imagined rage flickering inside her. Left alone all this time. Hatred and longing. Of thee we sing.

And then, looking into Odie's bemused face, Ruth felt her life suddenly tick forward. She told Winnie how badly Odie's cracked lips needed salve. Scratches, some healed-over, ran down his face and arms. His hair, matted with dirt, leaves. Oh, he was a sight, *she said.*

What news did Odie bring?

He told Ruth, in his rasp, of the pain he had brought to others and of the hardships he'd endured. They say, do no harm, *he told her,* but how can you not?

When Odie spoke, did Ruth hear the drone of insects? Or the hum of things at work inside us, steadily doing and undoing?

Ruth told Winnie she made Odie a cup of Earl Gray Tea. That she listened, enchanted. It was like a spell, *Ruth said.* As if he were telling my own story.

Yes. Our own story.

Odie told Ruth how years ago, a former patient of his injured her head in a car accident. Diffuse axonal injury, Odie said. Nasty blow. She went into a vegetative state for two years. All that time, her husband had to feed and bathe her. The poor bugger finally had to quit his job, Odie said. Farm his little ones out to his parents. The best nuerologists recommended institutionalizing the woman. Steady decline, they told the husband. But the husband wouldn't have it. Then one day, no different than all the others, the husband was spoon-feeding the woman and she woke up. Her eyes focused. She looked at her husband. Then turned her head to see out the window. She said to him, When I see that fig tree out our bedroom window, I think, *I am home.*

We, too, looked out that window. Saw that tree.

And then

Acknowledgements

Tommi Ferguson generously gave her heart and mind to this project from its start in 1999 to its final edits. My daughters, Ellie and Ava Blackwood, contributed their patience, love, beauty, and smarts; my brother, Dean, understood the vision for the book and held me to the task; Scott Stebler lent me his critic's eye and his expertise as a probate attorney; Rosa Eberly was a force of kairos, insight, and support. And my parents, Anita & Bob Gatchel and Bill & Lois Blackwood, contributed their love and support, through thick and thin.

Others who helped along the way (in no particular order): Michele Solberg, Debra Monroe, John Ruszkiewicz, Lester Faigley, Mike Hennessey, Tom Grimes, Kathie Lang, Kirsten Siegfried (for her wonderful Alaska stories), Katherine and Charles Ferguson; Allison Perlman, Michael Adams, Audrey Slate, Eliana Schonberg, Marianne Swierenga, Natalie Giarratano, Sue Mendelsohn, Ellen Crowell, Susan Briante, Kurt Heinzelman, Kevin Grauke, Julie Chibbaro, Madison Searle, Laurie, Emma, and Iris Blackwood, Christine Blackwood (Nana), Garrett Gatchel, Tim, Susan, and Will Taunton, Terry Dalrymple, Alex Parsons, Johan Hofzinzer, David McGlynn, Laura Furman, Jim Magnuson, Jim Sanderson, Dave Hamrick, Evan Carton, Mark Busby, Dana Stebler, John Lemaux, Carol

Dawson, Pat Beach, Mike O'Conner, Jon Burnett, Jodi Daynard, Prudence Arceneaux, Claire Jones, Jonathan Davis, Jeff Salamon, Jeff Tweedy and Wilco, Michael Erard, Kim Kupperman, Jill Meyers, Paige Normand, Frank Kermode (for *The Sense of an Ending*), Carol Reed (for *The Third Man*), Annie Dillard, Julie Gray, Shawn Badgley, Mary Ramsey, Luke Bilberry, Jen Adams, Linda Germain, Dale Smith, Robert Eversz, Suloni Robertson, Andre Dubus, Orson Welles, Sir Lionel Luckhoo, John Fahey, James Still, Gabriel Garcia Márquez, Ray Carver, Lawrence Weschler, Herman Melville (for his "botching"), William Faulkner, Flannery O'Conner, Alice Munro, Stuart Dybek, the New Grape Twins, my UT creative writing students, the Austin History Center, the Dobie Ranch, Amanda Schwarz, Tricia Hennessy, Paul Sizer, Owen Egerton, Yaphet Smith, Paige Normand, Noel Wagner and Charisse Kelly and the Deep Eddy Neighborhood of Austin, Texas.

In memory of my grandparents, Bill and Dean Taunton & Dewey Blackwood.

Thanks to the Association of Writers and Writing Programs (AWP), New Issues Press, Texas Commission on the Arts, The Writers League of Texas, The Texas Institute of Letters, UT's Undergraduate Writing Center, The University of Texas at Austin, and the Dobie Paisano Fellowship for their generous support.

A special thanks to the Roosevelt University community for their warm welcome.

photo by Tommi Ferguson

Scott Blackwood's award-winning collection of stories, *In the Shadow of Our House,* was published by SMU Press in 2001. His fiction has appeared in *American Short Fiction, Gettysburg Review, Boston Review* and *Southwest Review*, and the title story from his collection is featured on the *New York Times* Book Review's "First Chapters" website. Blackwood has won a Dobie Paisano Fellowship, two Texas Commission on the Arts Fellowships, and twice been nominated for the Pushcart Prize. He is an Assistant Professor of English and Director of the MFA Program in Creative Writing at Roosevelt University, Chicago.